THE LAND, THE LAND

Robin Hawdon

Print ISBN 9780993356742

Published by
Llyfrau Cambria Books, Wales, United Kingdom.
Cambria Books is a division of
Cambria Publishing Ltd.
Discover our other books at: www.cambriabooks.co.uk

For my wife, who came from the land.

"The land is the only thing in the world worth working for, worth fighting for, worth dying for - because it's the only thing that lasts." - *Gone With The Wind*.

CONTENTS

CHAPTER ONE

I know why people die for their land.

I don't mean die for their country. I mean die for their *land*. I'd die for my land. I'd die for a single acre of my land. And I've got near a thousand of them.

A thousand wild, bucking, rolling, diving, cruel, angry, languid, tender, loving, magnificent acres – more beautiful and more brutal than you'll find anywhere. They rise from rich pastures along the valley where the river runs and our few cattle graze, up the hillsides where our several hundred sheep survive all weathers amongst the rocks and heather, then leaping fifteen hundred feet to the high fells, which belong to nobody except some billionaire grouse shooter, and where nothing endures except rabbits and snakes and a few mad hikers. I love them more than anything else. More than life, more than people, and as much as my family. Because they are my family. Without them my family wouldn't be here. Without them *I* wouldn't be here. I'd be lying in some gutter in some dirty town, pissed, drugged, useless. My land is me.

I know every stick and every stone. I know every contour of the heaving hills, every ripple of the streams, every branch on every tree, every trout's rock, every otter's cave, every fox hole, every plover's nest, every hawk's cloud, every mood.

I am my land. My land is me.

It was my dad's. And his dad's before him. And it will be my daughter's. I have a son but he's younger than her, and he couldn't farm it anyway. He's brain damaged. A touch daft as they say in Yorkshire. Not severely, but enough to stop him doing the stuff that's necessary. But my daughter's as good as a son. Not to look at her. She's slim and svelte as a willow stem, but underneath as tough as any biker thug. You don't mess with her. Mess with her and you'll end up with a pea-soup brain if it's mental, and searing balls if it's physical. A lot of the local lads have tried. They've all been sent on their way. She knows what she wants, and it's not a Yorkshire farm boy. And it's not

1

what I want for her.

My son can produce puzzles from his strange brain that would fox Einstein, and my daughter can ride a horse like a Wild West rodeo girl. Glued to the saddle, swinging with the animal like it's part of her. She'll always take the horse to move the sheep or bring in the cows, rather than take the jeep or the land buggy. She and her mare will go up Shere Fell like it was a hiccup on a racetrack, with Trigger the sheep dog sprinting to keep up. They'll leap a gully or a dry-stone wall like it's a grass tuft. Doesn't matter how often we tell her not to, she'll still jump everything. Thank God we got her a good horse. Chardonnay, she called it – Shard for short - because that's its colour. And Shard loves jumping things as much as she does. She's the best horse woman in a county full of horse women. And Chardonnay's one of the best trained horses. But then they had a good teacher. Me.

And she loves the land as much as I do. Never welded to her smart phone like all her classmates, numbing their brains and blinding their eyes. And to do him credit so does my son. He can't go round the farm like she does, not unless one of us takes him in the buggy, but it's there in his soul. She'll go out in all weathers, all seasons, but he'll just sit on the porch or in his bedroom window, one of the farm cats on his lap, looking after her as she gallops off. Then watching out for the sheep, the birds, the beasts – anything that moves. Including the sky and the foaming grasses. He has binoculars and he keeps notebooks full of the stuff that's going on out there, although only he can read them. None of us can interpret his scrawls. But an environmentalist could learn a lot if he could read them. He is simpleton and sage in one body.

Still, being young, neither of the kids have the endless patience with the land that I do. In the evenings they and their mother will be playing fierce card games, or chattering. Or watching the soaps and the game shows on TV. I never saw the attraction in all that stuff. And the adverts make me want to throw things. No, I'll be out on the porch with Trigger, watching the sun go down over the western ridge, and listening to the snipes drumming. Or of it's too cold to sit, we'll wander down to the valley meadows to see if the grass is still growing

2

and the river still running. There is serenity in watching nature do nothing. Trigger and me can stand and watch water run or a tree grow for hours. We can watch a cow grazing and tell you to the nearest pound how much grass it gets through in half an hour. We can tell you the exact times the fish will start to jump for the evening insect hatch, the heron goes home for the night, the barn owls start their hunt. We can hear if a sheep is having trouble in labour a mile away, or a fox is giving it to his missus. We can smell the universe in the night.

My wife doesn't have the land in her bones in the same way. She comes from town stock – cars and pavements and tidy gardens. She's a smart city girl, with culture in her blood rather than nature. But she accepts it because she knows there's no other way. I met her at a posh function in York, and loved her at first sight and my hormones and me wouldn't take no for an answer. I dragged her off from her sophisticated university professor's home, and her shops and theatres and restaurants, and I brought her here to the wilds seventy miles away. She came because she loved me too, and because her hormones wouldn't take no for an answer either. But it wasn't what she would have chosen. It took her a while to get used to the huge, heavy silence of the land. And the huge, heavy sounds. She likes it when it's pretty and warm and sunny, and when she can tend the peonies and the raspberries in the garden, but she doesn't love it when it's vicious and dark and flailing under the wind, like we do. She likes it when she can rock in the hammock under the copper beech, not when she has to plough through two feet of snow to bring the shopping in. She likes it when it's Mozart, not when it's Wagner.

And she's always a bit nervous. Always underneath a little bit scared of the dangers. Scared for herself and for her son. Doesn't show it but I know it's there. Because there are dangers. Dangers from storm and whirlwind. From falling rocks and tearing waters. From stampeding animals and clattering machinery.

Danger from people.

One of those is our neighbour. Brad Faulkner. He farms over the western fell, a mile as the crow flies, four miles by road. He's a mean one. Bad farmer. Always looking to supplement his struggling flock with other people's sheep. He'll steal them at a cricket's click, soon as your back is turned. Doesn't give a damn about die stains or ear tags, he'll find a way. Have them whisked off to slaughter, ready or not, and people in London are having them for Sunday lunch before you even know they're gone.

Then there's government danger. Wanting to put through roads going from somewhere to nowhere. Wanting to dam the river because there's not enough water in a county where it rains enough to drown a herd of elephants. Wanting to put up a forest of wind turbines because they think the skyline's too bare and needs decorating. Always wanting to interfere with the natural order.

Then there's big business. Wanting to dig mines because we've got some of the best stone and minerals in the world. Wanting to plant pine forests because the whole planet wants houses. Wanting to bring Arab sheiks to shoot anything that moves anywhere in sight.

Never mind danger from all the rest, who just want to tramp everywhere, wrecking the gates and the fences, stampeding the sheep, leaving their trash to fertilise the ground with plastic and aluminium.

Yes, people are the worst.

But I manage to see them all off. Mostly. They get the message that I'll kill for my land.

For instance, the other morning. It started just like any other day. I was over in the far meadows in the buggy, checking the gates and fences after a stormy April night. Leave the slightest hole in a fence, and the sheep will be through it in a trice, the calves will nose it big enough for a bus to get through, or the foxes will be creating genocide in the chicken runs. Only Trigger was with me. I often take my son because he loves to ride in the buggy, but this time I didn't take him, even though he screamed and shouted, because I had it filled with wire and posts and stuff.

Then, while I was fixing an old gate for the umpteenth time, Trigger growled. I followed his stare and noticed figures high up in the sheep pastures. Just two of them. Didn't look like hikers. One of them standing at the side of a track, the other actually balanced on

4

top of the dry-stone wall alongside, with binoculars. Both peering out across the valley. How did they get there, I thought? Half a mile off the lane, and in town clothes. We often get trespassers, but usually just idiot walkers lost their way. These were different. Then I noticed the car further back. Black saloon. The buggers had opened a gate and driven through.

I whistled to Trigger to jump in the back of the buggy, and drove straight up the hillside to where they stood. They saw me coming, and the one with binoculars jumped down from the wall, bringing a top stone thudding down with him. When I got close I could see they were proper city types. Dark suits, ties, black shoes. The one on the wall a good-looking youngish bloke around thirty. The other older, solider, greying hair. They smiled as I drew up beside them. False friendly – I didn't trust them as far as an Iraqi with a backpack. And I've met some of those.

'This is private property,' I said, stopping the buggy a yard from running them down.

'Oh, yes... sorry,' the younger one said. He was still smiling and his accent wasn't Yorkshire. Southerner probably. 'We just wanted to see the view from here. Beautiful valley.'

'It's still private,' I said, staying on the buggy. 'How d'you get in?'

'We, er...' He pointed back up the track. 'Well, I'm afraid we opened the gate. Naughty of us, but we didn't know how far along we'd have to come to see the view.'

'There's views all over the Dales. Why d'you want to see this one?'

The older man spoke. He was heavy jawed with thick eyebrows. Looked like a judge, or a business boss. He couldn't have climbed the wall even if he'd wanted to. 'No particular reason. It just looked a good route for a hike. We're planning a walking holiday, you see, and we got a bit lost finding the direction.'

Walking holiday my backside. 'There's plenty of hiker's maps for the area. You can find them in the village or online. They tell you how to avoid private property. Where to find the proper trails.'

'Yes, yes,' he grunted. Deep upmarket voice. 'Yes, we do have a map. We just missed our way a bit.'

A curlew's cry echoed far across the hillside. I noticed it but they didn't. It was calling its mate – 'catch me if you can'. I pointed at the wall. 'That's loose stones, you know. Been there two hundred years. Takes a lot of skill to build that.'

'Ah, yes,' said the other. He looked contrite, false or genuine, I couldn't tell. 'Sorry. I won't make that mistake again.' All charm and blue eyes. I was glad my daughter wasn't with me.

'Well, be sure to close the gate when you get back to the road. The sheep need any excuse.'

'Of course.' He hesitated. 'Are you the farmer here?'

Stupid question. 'Yes.'

'Nice property. How many acres?'

Hello, what was he after? 'A thousand.'

'All up the valley there? Both sides of the river?'

'Yes.'

He nodded. 'Beautiful. You're not a tenant farmer.'

He said it as though he knew the answer. I shook my head. 'Been in my family for a hundred years.' I was uneasy. I was never easy with smart-collar business types like these two. I met up with such sometimes, usually when I went to London on Farmers Union business, and I could handle those discussions all right, but I always felt we were speaking different languages. I always came away feeling that we were two different species. Feeling town and country could never really mix. Just as Pekingese and Fox Hounds don't mix.

A gust of wind spoiled their haircuts. The day was dancing like a street rapper. 'Well, thank you for warning us,' he said. 'Sorry to be trespassing. We'll get out of your way now.'

They went to their car. The wind followed, speeding them up.

'You won't be able to turn there,' I called. 'You'll need to back up the track.'

'Oh, right.'

They got in quickly, as though the breeze carried typhoid. The young one was driving. Smart Audi model. He backed it up the track, bumping over the ruts. Serve them right if they went over the edge, I thought. Walkers my bollocks.

'What did you think of them. Trigger?' I said.

He was a Border Collie – sharp as a whistle, brightest breed on the planet. He was nine years old, but had a good few in him yet. He could round up a hundred sheep in ten minutes. He wagged his tail, saying 'Bugger them – what's for lunch?'

We went back to the house, and I thought little more of it. Except in the night. Then I lay awake in the sweeping black, wondering. What did they want?

'What's the matter?' Annie mumbled beside me. Her long brown hair was spread over the pillows. Almost in my face, but I didn't mind. I liked the smell of it. Hay and baking and shampoo.

'Oh nothing. Just me. Thinking as usual.'

'Go to sleep.'

That's the trouble. Whether it's strange visitors, or uncertain weather, or fractious animals, I invariably found it hard to sleep. Too many imaginings in the dark. But that's farming for you. You never know what's round the corner.

I'd learnt that the hard way. I've only got one arm. Because I didn't know what was round the corner.

CHAPTER TWO

munday. 11.42. temp 24C. sun and ciris clowds. lot of swolows and a
kestril and 9 rabits in the buloks feeld. dad going to markit tomorow
hope he teks me. gografy leson with dad we lernd abowt animels in africa.
they are bigger than owrs espshly the girafs. beef stuw for diner tonite and
trecil tart my no 3 favrit. do my insec jar now caught anuther cricit for it

Two weeks later I got a phone call. I could not have known it would change all our lives. But then lives often change on a coin spin.

I'd already had the full carbohydrate breakfast, cooked by Annie, even though she only had muesli and orange juice herself. Have a proper breakfast and the day will take care of itself, my father always said. I'd brought in the cows for milking, and left them to old Jim, our farm hand. He'd started with my grandfather, worked all through my father's days, and now worked for me. He was as much a part of the farm as were the cows, and he was happier with cows than with people.

I was in the middle of doing a home lesson with my disabled son – geography, an easy one because he loved it – when the landline rang.

'Is that Mr Oldfield?' It was a female voice, posh and professional.

'Yes,' I said.

'Oh, good morning. I'm Denise Armstrong, personal assistant to Mr Collins, the CEO of Dragonsmead Holdings.' She said it as if it was the Bank of England and I'd know who they were.

'Who are they?'

'We're a company based in London.'

'I haven't heard of them.'

'No – well, we're only a few years old. An amalgamation of several firms, but quite a big company. We deal in property, resources, mining, transport. Many things.'

'Ah.' I was thinking, she's got the wrong number.

'Mr Collins wants to meet you.'

'Why?'

'He wants to discuss something with you. A business proposal.'

'Business?'

'Yes.'

'My farm isn't for sale.'

'No, it's nothing like that. It's a proposition.' She made it sound like a proposal of marriage.

'Why would he want to discuss business with me?'

'Well, of course I'm not at liberty to talk about the details over the phone, but he wondered whether you'd like to come to London to meet him. We'd pay all expenses of course, and put you up in a hotel if you wished to stay the night.'

I was quiet. What the hell was this? Had I won Farmer of the Year or something?

'Mr Oldfield? Are you still there?'

'I don't come to London very often.'

'No, I realise it's a long way. But there's a very good train service. It's only two hours or so from Darlington. We'd email you a first class ticket. And we'll pick you up at the other end.'

I put the phone to my other ear. Perhaps I'd hear more sense there. Danny's lip was protruding. He didn't like losing my attention.

'Well... I don't know. Can't he come to me?'

'Um... not really. He has things he wants to show you. Not the sort of stuff you can take on a train.'

New tractor model? Pedigree bull for sale? I said, 'Can I speak to him?'

'It's a bit difficult. He's in a meeting now, and he has a full schedule. But I assure you it's on quite an important matter.'

'I'm right in the middle of the lambing season.'

'Oh, yes of course. That must be a busy time for you.'

'It is.'

'Do you have many lambs coming?'

9

'A good few. About fifteen million country wide.'

'Goodness! That many? I never realised.'

A real London lass. 'No, well you can see how difficult it would be.'

'When does the lambing finish?'

'A couple of weeks probably.' I didn't say we were already nearly done.

'Oh, well I'm sure Mr Collins can wait that long. Shall I give you two weeks and then call back again?'

'Yes, that would be the best thing.'

'Very well. It's been so nice talking to you, Mr Oldfield. I hope the lambing goes well.'

I sat there, thinking. What was this about? London businessmen? I'd have bet a pea to a pork pie it had something to do with those two characters I'd seen up on the track.

Danny and Trigger were watching me. Danny impatient, Trigger alert. He knew something was up.

'What's going on, Trigger?' I muttered.

He cocked his ears. He'd have told me if he could. Then my father shuffled into the room. He asked the same question. 'What's goin' on?'

Dad was well into his seventies and lived with us since Mum died, but in his own small wing at the back of the house. It used to be the dairy long ago, before we built the modern one across the farmyard. Now it was a tidy little self-contained unit, opening onto the back garden. He didn't keep it very tidy, but he pottered about doing his own thing, and popping in from time to time to check on the rest of us. He was a grizzled old bugger, half-hobbled now with arthritis, and didn't think much of today's world. But he had loved the land as much as I did, and didn't have many regrets. He and I maintained a wary relationship. He'd been pretty tough on me and my sister as a father, but he taught me all I knew. It was him who developed the dairy herd from the few cows his father had left behind. 'Always keep cows,' he used to say. 'They're more daily work than sheep, but they keep the balance in a farm. You need them to keep the grass good.

10

You need the manure for everywhere else. You need them for when the sheep let you down.' The family used to joke that he loved his cows more than us. Certainly my sister left home as soon as she could, to get away from his bullying. She went to York and became an estate agent, whilst I took over the farm. My dad never showed he missed her, but I noticed that he always listened in when she rang about something.

He may have relinquished the reins, but he didn't miss much. Now he had sensed that something was up, and he wanted to know. So I told him.

He grunted, scratched his chest, and growled, 'Uhuh. Business people. You want to watch them, son. If they've got interest, you can be blurry sure it won't be in your interest.'

Always the cynic, my dad. He went off again. But I knew he'd be thinking about it, and would come back with it later. He never let anything go.

'Can we do my lesson now?' said Danny. He was more interested in African wildlife then big business.

In fact any kind of wildlife. He knew more facts about the animal and insect world than any of us. He kept a regular diary. It was almost impossible to read, but apart from his nature notes I suspected it chronicled things about us and the farm that might have bewildered us. Or amused. Or maybe just embarrassed. Astonishingly, he also liked music. Classical music. Only three pieces, but he played them over and over through his headphones. The only other music he liked was Abba. And bagpipes.

I'd often talk to him about stuff, and even if he didn't understand it all he'd sometimes come out with an off-the-wall idea that brought me up short. He went to a special school two days a week. It was a long taxi ride away and we couldn't afford more, but they were good for him. I always wanted what was good for him. Because I always felt it was my fault.

Two weeks later, on the dot, she rang again. 'How's the lambing going, Mr Oldfield?'

11

'Fine.'

'That's good. So might you be free to come to London? Say the beginning of next week?'

I had thought a lot about it over the fortnight. Talked it over with Annie. I couldn't see a way out of it. Besides I was curious. I knew there was a whole world out there that I ought to know more about.

'Yes, all right.'

'Oh, that's good. Mr Collins will be delighted. Shall we say Monday afternoon? I'll email you a ticket for the morning train, we'll pick you up at the station, and we'll schedule a meeting for two o'clock at our offices. Would you like a hotel for the night?'

'Yes, please.' Buggered if I was going to do that journey twice in a day.

'Splendid. I'll send you all the details.'

I could do with someone like her running the farm business. Far too much bloody bureaucracy these days. My grandfather never had to deal with all that. Just got on rearing the sheep and milking the cows and loving the land. Annie did the accounts, and she was good. But it was a chore, as was all the government paperwork. Nothing to do but make work for people, these civil servants. And I bet none of them knew one end of a Swaledale sheep from another.

We talked it over at dinner that evening. Big family time - dinner. The huge kitchen table had an eye-dazzling tablecloth over it which Annie had picked up in the Mediterranean somewhere, and there were five of us, including my dad, who joined us from time to time. We'd had a dozen round it before. A chilly evening, but the granite walls of the farmhouse, thick as a pig, kept the wind out, and the big old Aga spewed its heat all round the house. We had the last of the caid lambs in the warming oven after a difficult birth. The cats were curled on the big leather sofa, half a century old. Spiders hung in the ceiling corners, playing their everlasting waiting game. Even Trigger was allowed in on cold nights. The womb of the house I always thought the room was.

Annie was dishing out the shepherd's pie (what else?). She made a terrific shepherd's pie, better than any you could get in the pub. It had

12

a secret ingredient, but no one ever found out what it was. 'What do you think they want?' she said.

'Haven't the foggiest,' I said. 'What could we have that they want? There's no industrial value here. No coal in the ground, no minerals. I can't think they're into farming sheep.' I looked at my father, who was sipping at his regular half-pint of brown ale. 'What do you think, Dad?'

He used his dog growl voice. 'Dunno, but don't trust 'em. These big corporations are takin' over the whole bloody world.' He glowered into his glass. 'They'll give you all the smooth talk, but they'll skin you alive soon as they get the chance.'

'Oh, Dad,' said Annie, 'don't be so suspicious.'

He grunted and swallowed his beer.

Lily, my daughter, piling peas onto the plates, said, 'Perhaps they want to build an airport here. Or a golf course. Or a holiday resort.'

Always big ideas, Lily. I threw her a look. 'Not likely. They can't build here anyway. Area of natural beauty.'

'Could they plant anything?' said Annie. 'Timber? Crops?'

'Cannabis,' said Lily, grinning.

'What's canna piss?' asked Danny.

She giggled and ruffled his hair, which he hated. 'It's nasty stuff that stops you peeing. That's why it's called that.'

'The only thing I can think of,' I said, 'is putting a dam at the head of the valley and turning it into a lake.'

'What for?' asked Annie.

'Reservoir. Global warming, droughts.'

She snorted. 'Not much drought around here.'

'No, but preparing for the future.'

Dad shook his head. 'That would be a government thing. Or local water company. Not a London outfit.'

I agreed. 'I'm foxed.'

Danny spoke in his mangled nasal voice, which some found hard to understand. 'I know what it is.'

'What, Danny?'

He was shovelling pie into his mouth. Appetite like King Kong,

Danny. 'They want to put a safari park here. Lions and giraffes. Crocodiles in the river.'

Lily clapped her hands. 'Great idea, Danny. I'd go for that.'

Annie drooped her eyelids at me. 'You must stop teaching him about Africa.'

'Well, that would be better than high-rise flats,' I said.

'You could get a lot of animals into a high-rise flat,' said Danny.

The candles flickered on the table. Annie liked to have candles at dinner-time. The sort of touch my family rarely considered. It was her cultured background again, and one of the things I loved about her. She brought the refinements to life that I admired, but never had time for.

I poured myself some more wine with my good arm. The other's only half there – useful for pushing, but no good for holding. I always tried to limit my drinking, but usually failed.

'We'll just have to wait till Monday,' I said.

Lily held out her glass for some. She was allowed a glass. 'Can I come with you?' she said, fair head on one side.

I stared. 'To London? Why?'

'I've only been there twice. I want to see it.'

I looked at Annie. 'Would it matter?'

'She's got school. It's her final year. Exams.'

I wanted her to get those, but I also liked the idea of having her to myself for a bit. 'A couple of days wouldn't matter. We'd say she's caught cold.'

'Yes!' Lily exclaimed. 'I'll catch up lessons – no problem.'

'Well...' Annie hesitated.

Lily clapped her hands again. 'Good. That's settled. I can stay in the hotel with Dad.'

'Can I come?' said Danny.

I smiled at him. 'You wouldn't like it, Danny. Noise and traffic and far too many people.'

He was happy with that. 'Yeh – nine million, four hundred thousand in London.' He held out his plate for more.

'Would Lily go to the meeting?' asked Annie. We had always

brought her in on everything to do with the farm.

I thought about it as I pulled a sliver of sheep bone out of my mouth, which had nearly cracked a tooth. To have her there felt right, if only for the moral support. 'I don't see why not,' I said.

Lily smiled. The idea didn't scare her.

'Good,' said my dad. 'Give her a taste of the business world.' That made a change, coming from him. 'Then she'll see what it's like.'

'What's for pudding?' said Danny.

The emails with the train ticket and the company address had come through. Also the hotel. Smart one in Park Lane. They were really trying to impress. I didn't fancy phoning them about Lily - don't like phones anyway. I emailed back. 'Would you mind if my daughter came with me? She's part owner of the farm, and I'd like her at the meeting.'

Another train ticket came through shortly. And another hotel room booked. This was a big thing for them.

'Wow!' said Lily. 'D'you think they could get us to meet the Queen?'

CHAPTER THREE

toosday. 20.16. temp 18C. in bed. shepids pie for diner and lemin tart
my no 4 favrit. dad and lil goin to lundun to morow to see peepil who
wont to bild stuf in owr farm. dad nervis abowt meetings like that but
lily not nervis about any thing. i wud be nervis but if it meens we had a
zoo we cud hav more animels. id speshly like to have some girafs they are
mi favrit animels. i think animels are niser than peeple they dont be rood
to me like peeple. ownly my famly and jim arnt rood. and my teechers at
my speshil scool. my cricits wer ded in my insec jar this morning. cricits
must be free like burds

I have to admit, despite my love affair with my land, I do get a
perverse thrill the occasional times I go to London. There is a side of
me that knows I'm missing other dimensions of life because of my
farmer's obsession. My trips are usually on Farmer's Union stuff, or
a rare culture holiday for Annie. Give her an art gallery visit and a
theatre show and she's happy for months. She always wants the
National Gallery and the National Theatre. I prefer the Natural
History Museum and a musical, but I usually give in in the end. None
of those this time though.

Lily and I didn't talk much as we sat in our first-class seats
watching the countryside rocket past, but it was nice having her there
beside me. Half of England swept by in two hours - hills to valleys,
rocks to woods, fields to houses, savage to gentle. We felt the
adrenalin rise as the train bore into the capital. It pierced the miles of
dull suburbs – people living like battery hens – then snaked in
amongst the high-rise flats, the lumped business blocks, and

eventually the shiny towers of the city centre. From ancient squalor to modern extravaganza in the length of my valley. The temperature rose literally and metaphorically as we walked down the wide platforms of King's Cross and headed for the roar outside. Lily felt it too. Her back straightened and her long legs strode longer as the vibrations of the place entered her spirit. She'd let her fair hair down and wore a rare swinging frock as she marched beside me, and she got quite a few looks from the fellas on the way.

We came out from the platforms, and the maelstrom of London hit us. Traffic like a herd stampeding, noise of six orchestras tuning up, a river of people rushing over rapids. And the smell and the noise together like being locked inside a tractor engine. How do people live with it, I wondered? Lily's eyes glowed. She loved it.

We reached the outer pickup area as instructed, and there sure enough was a black monster of a car, like an oversized beetle, with a grey uniformed chauffeur standing by it holding an open iPad with the words 'M & Ms Oldfield' in big letters. Welcome to the tycoons' world. I was glad I'd put on my only dark suit. My empty sleeve was stuck into my side pocket, and I had a tie in my other pocket, but I saved it till later. They're only good for keeping the soup stains off your shirt.

The driver introduced himself as Harry, the company chauffeur. He was a stocky Londoner of indeterminate age - one of the army of stoical employees on which the metropolis depends for its functioning. They soldier on, day after day, thinking of who knows what, and rarely get any thanks. He took our bags and opened the rear door of the car for us, people staring as if it was the Prime Minister's. We climbed into a space bigger than Lily's school bus, with more cream leather and suede and pile carpet around than a Hollywood tart's bedroom. As we glided off, space craft headed for the moon, Harry said in a cheerful London accent, 'I'm instructed to take you to your hotel, sir, where you can find your rooms, settle in, and have a spot of lunch. Then I'll pick you up again at a quarter to two, and take you to the offices of Dragonsmead. They're in Mayfair, not far from your hotel.'

17

'Fine,' I said, trying to sound as if it was an everyday experience. Lily said nothing, just raised an eyebrow at me, twinkling.

We drove south through the city, and the streets got ever ritzier, the buildings grander, until we reached Marble Arch, then down Park Lane, past the plane trees exploding spring green, to the hotel. More uniforms, more door openings, more bowing and scraping, and we were finally in our high adjoining rooms, bags carried in by a lackey, who explained all the lighting and air conditioning and electric blinds and TV controls – more complicated than a jet plane cockpit.

'Is there a button for automatic toilet paper?' I asked.

Lily snorted. He didn't get the joke. He glanced at my empty sleeve, then quickly away as people do, and left.

We stood staring out over the wide spaces of Hyde Park – countryside in the city.

'Almost as good as the forty acre field,' I said.

'Not quite,' Lily said. 'Missing a few animals and cow pats.'

'Yes. They should put some cattle in there, or perhaps a flock. Save them a hell of a lot of mowing.'

We ordered a light lunch from room service. Didn't want to face big dining rooms and hovering waiters. Sat in the window of my room, and got into prawn salads decked out like herbaceous borders, but quite tasty.

'I could take to this,' said Lily, sitting back with her coke in hand. 'D'you think they'd let us stay a week or two?'

'Maybe. Depends how badly they want what it is they want. We might be able to blackmail them.'

So then we were driven to the offices. Why we needed the car, I didn't know, since they were only a ten minute walk away, and with the traffic walking would have been quicker. The pavements breathed money. The company was in one of the high period terraces that line the streets of Mayfair – lots of grey stone and brass bells and doormen. Rent paid to the Duke of Westminster about a million an hour. We were met in the marble foyer by a seriously smart woman in black suit and high heels. That was all right, I had my tie on now.

'So glad you could get here,' she said smiling like the Mona Lisa.

'I'm Denise, Mr Collins's PA. We spoke on the phone.'

'Yes, of course,' I said, not to be outdone. 'Roger Oldfield. This is my daughter, Lily.'

'Charming.' We all shook hands, me twisting my hand backwards to do so, because it's on the left. 'Is your hotel all right?'

'Splendid.'

'Oh good. Well, we'll take the lift. He's on the top floor.'

We sailed up, silent as a church, some sort of perfume in the air – then along a carpeted corridor, past doors with phones ringing behind, and into an office as wide as my hay barn. Thick pile and glass windows and pictures of smart buildings and factories on the walls. A big man in a grey suit sat behind the desk, and a younger one stood staring out of the window. Even from the back I knew who he was.

'Here they are, Mr Collins,' said the woman.

The older man got up, smiling. He wasn't the one who had trespassed on the farm. He was almost as tall as me, and considerably heavier. In his late fifties I guessed. Probably played rugby once. He came forward, hand turned to take mine. He already knew apparently.

'I'm George Collins. I'm so grateful to you for making this trip. Must have been quite an inconvenience for you.'

'Not really,' I said, shaking his hand and matching him with the power squeeze. 'This is my daughter, Lily.'

'Delighted,' he said, expensive teeth glowing. 'And this is my son, Martin. I believe you've met.'

The blue eyes smiled and the natural teeth flashed. 'Under more awkward circumstances,' he said. 'I apologise again for my intrusion.'

I waved it away, and he turned his attention to Lily. 'So pleased to meet you.'

I watched her reaction. She gave him her nicest smile, but I could see she wasn't seduced. Not yet.

'Well,' said his father, 'let's all sit over here.' He indicated a seating area at the other end of the room – leather sofas the size of coal barges, marble coffee table you could skate on. 'Can I offer you something? Drink, tea, coffee?'

'We've just had a nice lunch at the hotel, thank you.'

'Oh, good. Well, do have a nice dinner there too. Anything you wish. It's all taken care of.'

'Thank you.'

He nodded at his PA. 'Thank you, Denise. I'll let you know if we need anything.'

She left, trailing efficiency. The two men sat opposite us. The sofas sighed.

'You'll be wondering what the hell this is all about.' His voice was deep, back in the throat, no accent.

'You could say that,' I replied.

He threw a quick glance at his son, then looked up at the patterned ceiling for a few seconds. Didn't find anything there, so looked back. 'Do you know what this building is built of, Roger. May I call you that?'

'Yes. Er... no, I don't. Limestone, I suppose'

'Yes, limestone. Like much of Mayfair. Like Buckingham Palace, St Paul's Cathedral.' He raised his thick eyebrows. 'The Pyramids of Giza.'

'Oh. Interesting.'

'Do you know what is the best limestone in Britain?'

'Portland?'

'Yes, Portland. Very expensive. Do you know where the next best limestone comes from?'

I pondered. 'My region, I imagine. The Pennines.'

'Exactly. It's coming right back into fashion, limestone. People are getting tired of glass and steel. They want the more traditional look. The stately homes of England are mostly built of limestone.' He waited. Silence. I waited too. I wasn't sure what was expected of me. Was he going to build a stately home? Then he put his big hands together. 'Have you heard of the Stainbridge Quarry?'

'Um... yes. Disused quarry about eight miles west of us.'

'That's right. Closed about seventy years ago, I believe.'

'Yes.' It was a grim place, home to occasional gypsy camps and teenage drug parties.

'They ran out of good stone. Too inaccessible. Couldn't dig down very far in those days.'

I waited again. The faint hum of traffic strummed from below, air conditioning hummed from above.

He went on. 'The thing about Stainbridge is that it's actually on a large seam of top quality limestone. Quite deep down, but stretching hundreds of metres. Beautiful pale stone, enough to build a city.'

'Really.'

'With modern mining methods that becomes much more accessible. It's the sort of product my company is very interested in. We do a lot of building, you see. Lot of construction. Prestige buildings. Material supplies. International contracts.'

'Ah.' I crossed my legs as though this was the sort of conversation I was used to.

'We've been looking into the possibilities of reopening Stainbridge. Fortunately it's just outside the protected area so it wouldn't be too difficult. And it's isolated, so not too many environmental problems.'

'Oh.'

'We've been negotiating with the present owners – Blackall Quarries, quite a large mining outfit – and we have an option to buy.' He pursed his lips. He seemed to be finding it all a bit difficult. I was happy not to help him out. 'But there's one big problem.'

'What's that?'

'Access. Or rather means of transport. Very heavy stuff, stone. A truck can only take twelve to fifteen tons. We want to shift a thousand tons a week. That's about seventy truckloads. All over the Yorkshire roads. Not feasible. So...' He looked at his son.

'So the only alternative is rail,' the young man said.

I was still none the wiser. I waited some more.

His father went on. 'A freight train could carry that much in one go. Flat-bed wagons. Eighty tons on each. But you see, there's no rail line close to the quarry. So we'd have to build our own.'

Things now sparked in my brain. I looked from one to the other.

The older man heaved himself out of his seat. 'We need to show you something. Come with us.' He led the way out of the office.

21

The four of us walked down the corridor to a door at the end. We went in. It was a smaller room, taken up largely with a three-dimensional landscape contour model sitting on trestles. There was barely room to move around the sides. It was made of papier-mâché or some such, pretty detailed. Showed hills and valleys, pastures and waterways spread over what must have been twenty miles square. Must have cost a fair bit to make.

They said nothing. I stared at it for several seconds. Then I realised where it was. The whole area of the Dales around home. With our valley bang in the middle of it.

I looked at Lily. She had recognised it too.

The boss man spoke. 'You see where this is?' I nodded. He pointed to the top end. 'There's the Stainbridge quarry.' He pointed off towards the other end. 'That's the direction of Darlington and the main rail network. Which is where we'd have to link into. Less than twenty miles, not too far. From there we can shift stone south and north. Off to the Midlands and the ports in every direction. Most of Britain in fact.'

I nodded, waiting for the time bomb. There was the muffled sound of a police siren from the street.

'Problem is there's mostly the high hills between us and there.' He threw me a glance and pointed again. I noticed the painted red line running from the quarry right to the edge of our land, then through the valley following the river, and curving off eastwards over the other boundary.

'The only feasible route is through your valley.'

You could have heard a chicken feather fall.

He waited. The seconds passed. When he realised he was going to get no reaction he said, 'I appreciate this is a big thing for you to take in. However it could be the makings of you and your family. We are prepared to make you an offer which would set you and your future generations up for life.' He glanced at his son, who was standing expressionless on the other side of the table. 'We are offering two million pounds for the right to run a single-track rail along that line, plus a toll on every wagon that passes. You would never have to work

22

again. You could sell all your sheep, and live a life of luxury.'

Funny. You would have thought a successful businessman would know what was the right and what was the wrong thing to say. You would think he might have done a bit of research into a potential partner in a big enterprise like that.

I looked him in the eye, but didn't say anything.

He blinked, then asked, 'Well, Roger, have you nothing to say?'

'Don't you need planning permissions or something for this?'

He smiled then, relieved that I could still talk. 'Ah, we've been into all that. We've talked to the local councils. And to the powers that be here in London. We have influence in quite high places. Of course it will bring a lot of employment and investment into the area. It shouldn't be a problem.' He moved to the end nearest the quarry, and pointed. 'You can see part of the route also crosses the corner of your neighbour's land.'

I looked. 'Faulkner's farm?'

'Yes.'

'Have you talked to him?'

'Not yet.'

'Well, good luck doing business with him.'

'Why?'

'Let's just say he's not to be trusted.'

He half smiled as if he already knew. 'We can handle him.'

Lily spoke. Her eyebrows were curled into question marks. 'It splits the farm in two. How would we get from one side to the other?'

'Oh, we've thought of that. We'd put a bridge across the culvert there. Close to your river bridge.' He watched our reaction again. When he didn't get one he added, 'Perhaps we might put another one up at the far end there.'

I said, 'A lot of expense. Is the quarry worth all that?'

'Yes. The potential is enormous.'

I nodded. 'Of course you could also build a station in the middle with a car park, so us and all the local people could get a lift on the wagons.'

He looked startled for a moment, then realised I was joking and guffawed loudly. 'Of course, Roger, of course. Anything you like.' He put a hand on my shoulder, and said, 'Let's go back to my office, and talk about it over a cup of tea. It's a lot to take in. You'll need time to assimilate it all. But this could be a huge opportunity. For you and for us.'

I don't remember much of the rest of the meeting. A lot of facts and figures. A lot of stuff about bringing the area into the twenty first century. A lot of environmental waffle. His son chimed in occasionally with comments. The elegant Denise came and went with dinky tea and biscuits, and files full of graphs and numbers. Then, when it seemed they had covered most things to their satisfaction, and handed us two glossy booklets showing it all again, the man said to me, 'What do you think you might do if we could pull this off, Roger? I know the farm has been with your family for a number of generations. Would you keep it going? Would you hand it over to a manager? Would you keep all your sheep and animals?'

I thought for a moment. I didn't want to hurt the man's feelings. After all, he probably loved his business as much as I did mine. So I said, 'I'll tell you something about sheep, Mr Collins. Something not many people realise.'

'What's that?'

'Without sheep you and I wouldn't be here. Without sheep you wouldn't have a business. Without sheep your fine limestone buildings would never have been built.'

He frowned, not understanding.

'People think the Industrial Revolution here in Britain was what made us great. Launched the British Empire, led the modern developed world. But in fact all that would never have happened if it wasn't for sheep. And for something that happened six hundred years earlier. Have you any idea what that was?'

He shook his head. He looked perplexed now, not a state he was used to I imagined.

'It was the extermination within these shores of the wolf.' I paused for effect. The pair of them were mesmerised. I went on. 'In medieval times wolves were the biggest enemy of domestic animals, and sheep were the most valuable of those animals. Because of the prevalence of great wolf packs across Europe, no one could maintain large sheep flocks. They had to be corralled and protected round the clock in modest numbers. But Britain – especially England – started to get on top of the problem in the twelfth and thirteenth centuries. The land owners, the aristocracy, and the king himself organised huge culls countrywide. Over a hundred years and more, the wolf population was virtually extinguished. This allowed the great expansion of sheep flocks all across this green and pleasant land. The rest of Europe couldn't match us, because the wolf packs marauding from the vast forests of Russia and the Baltics were just too numerous. And in any case their sheep species couldn't compete with the fine wool producing breeds that thrived in our temperate climate.'

They were staring at me as though I was explaining the Theory of Relativity.

'Britain became the wool producers for the world, clothing people from Scandinavia to Arabia, exporting pure wool to the cloth makers of Flanders and Florence. And of course she then had to create a merchant fleet to transport the magic stuff around. Then an armed navy to protect those ships from pirates and enemy assaults. Also a sophisticated banking system to handle all the business side of things. The whole system spread across the land. Your average sheep farmer like me became a man of means, and the large landowner a tycoon like you. And almost every historic building in Britain, from cathedrals to mills and manor houses, all mostly built of your limestone, were financed by the wealth produced by wool. And it was all this which, over the centuries, drove the culture of invention and exploration that eventually produced the Industrial Revolution.' I raised my cup of tea. 'Sheep!'

Yet another silence. Relativity had frozen their brains. Lily was studying her fingernails. She'd heard the sermon before.

Then Collins smiled, a rather tight smile. 'Well, that was wonderful, Roger. Remarkable. One learns something every day.' He raised his own cup to me. 'So you'll be able to breed more sheep. Buy up half of Yorkshire and put sheep all over it.'

We left then, with our glossy booklets. All smiles and politeness, and thank you for everything. 'Take a bit of time to think over it all,' they said, and 'Yes, of course we will,' we said, and 'We'll be in touch soon,' we all said.

Lily and I had dinner in the evening. I had planned to take her to a theatre or a cinema or something, but we weren't in the mood, so we just dined at the hotel since it was paid for. Sat in the aircraft-hangar dining room and had the most expensive dishes on the menu.

We were largely silent, staring into our wine glasses full of some smart French tipple. Waiters glided about on skates. Silver clinked on china. Smart men with smart women of a dozen different nationalities murmured around us like the hum of a beehive.

'What are you thinking, Dad?' she said.

'Don't know what to think. Don't know how to answer them. They're from another planet.'

'Are you tempted?'

'Lord no. Railway line through the farm? Can you imagine it? Like putting mustard in an apple pie.' I looked at her. 'What do you think?'

She shook her head. 'No. Can't imagine it.'

'Well, that's it then. Nice trip to London, and thank you very much – see you never.'

She grinned. A wide smile. Our young Italian waiter made a big show of topping up her wine glass.

CHAPTER FOUR

thirsday. 6.08. temp 19C. good its mi speshil scool day. i go to a speshil
scool becos i dont think lik uther peeple. i hav to lern sum things uther
peeple do but sum times i wish they cud think lik me. jo mi taxy man
and me talk a lot. he says he wud lik to think lik me sum times. he
askd me how my dad lost his arm. i sed it was an axydent but i didn no
he dusnt talk abowt it. jo sed life is ful of axydents

It happened two years after Danny was born. We were replacing an old steel water tank beside the milking parlour with a bigger modern one. We were always replacing something with something better. Jim was off somewhere, so Annie was working the forklift on the tractor whilst I guided her in. She was good at it. We'd lifted the old tank from the cement base, and set it aside. She was manoeuvring the new one in on the forks – big, ugly thing – a tricky business, lowering it precisely down onto the base as I bent low, hand signalling directions. Then, when the tank was about two feet above the concrete, I suddenly noticed an iron bracket from the old tank lying there, and put my hand underneath to grab it.

Stupid or daft? I knew the rules. I'd been told a thousand times by my father and my grandfather – always take precautions, always check, always look out for emergencies.

Whether it was that Annie hit the wrong lever, or simply that the old fork mechanism gave way under the weight, we never knew. But three hundred kilos of heavy plastic crashed down at that precise moment.

The last thing I heard before I blacked out was a thunderous crash, topped by Annie's scream.

I woke in hospital two days later, to see her gaunt, red-eyed face hovering over me. She looked far worse than I felt. I smiled, and she collapsed weeping onto my chest.

The doctors couldn't save the arm. The bone had been crushed below the elbow into a thousand fragments. Mincemeat, shepherd's pie. They cut it off at the joint, and saved the upper half. I was glad I'd been unconscious over the whole panicked rescue process and hospital operation. It had been much harder for her watching it all. She felt it was all her fault, although we never really knew how it happened.

I told her we were evens now. She'd survived the trauma of Danny, and I'd survived the trauma of losing an arm. She said they weren't the same thing. I said they were in a way. We both had to take responsibility for both challenges. That made her break down and cry again.

It had been my right arm, and it took me two years to get the left one up to the same strength and dexterity. Pathetic really. Nelson was back leading his men an hour after losing his. The insurance paid up a good sum, and the National Health provided a prosthetic arm, but I couldn't get on with it. Like trying to milk a cow with a spanner. I gave up after six months. Funnily enough the right stump proved quite useful, holding things down, pushing stuff around. After a while I got used to it. Even to all the jokes. 'D'you need a hand?', 'You're a one-arm bandit', 'One hand clapping', 'You're not fully armed for this job', and so on. Even Annie started to smile at them.

The kids were still little more than babies, so she had her own hands full looking after them, and filling in for me on the farm. Fortunately we had Jim and Doris, who were younger then, and brought four more hands to the job, and we hired in extra help. We suffered a bit that first year, but then I got back into form, and we were again operating at normal speed. The human body is extraordinary. Take whole components away, and it will still function.

It was a lesson though. From then on I planned things as if planning the Normandy invasion. I took ever more careful precautions against what fate might have in store. For the family and the farm more than myself.

Lily was the only one I could never tame. Lily rode her horse and climbed trees and fought the boys with an abandon that I couldn't educate. I had to simply warn her, and cross my fingers, and hope that she'd come out all right.

And Danny was beyond my protection in other ways. He either didn't understand, or forgot, or simply got so engrossed in his own projects that he lost all awareness of anything else.

And of course part of me admired them for it. You can't tame free spirits.

CHAPTER FIVE

tusday 10.53 clowdy sun, temp 23C. mum did scrambild egs for brekfist my number 2 favrit brekfist. peepil wont to bild a relway in the farm. i went on a relway with grampa it wos a steem train lik they use to hav lik the flying scots man wich cud go at 108 mils per owr. owrs only went at 48 mils per owr i no bicos i askd the train driver. dad dusnt wont a relway becos its noisy and ugly. i think relways can be ecsiting. but perhaps they dont go with animels and insecs. peepl sum times dont go with animels. insecs dont care abowt peeple

They say that Yorkshire folk are the most stubborn in the country. It's probably right. They've had to be to survive their history and the weather. But they're also some of the kindest.

My parents were the old-fashioned kind. They brought me up to always observe the niceties. Always say please and thank you, always open the door for a lady, always write thankyou letters to the uncles and aunts who sent birthday presents, and the mums who invited you to their kids' birthday parties.

I wrote to George Collins, care of Dragonsmead Holdings.

Dear Mr Collins,

Thank you so much for inviting my daughter and I to London, and for providing such pleasant accommodation. We enjoyed our trip very much.

And thank you also for your generous offer over rail transport rights through our land. I and my family discussed the proposal at great length. However we have decided that, tempting though your offer is, we must decline it for the sake of the farm and its functions, and for the preservation of our beautiful valley.

I do hope you understand.
Yours sincerely, Roger Oldfield.

I read it to Annie, and she suggested a few changes, and we agreed it would do. I thought it was a bit short, but she said, no, it was a business letter so didn't need embellishing. I sent it off, and got on with more important matters. Such as how to change a wheel on a trailer with a spanner, a hammer, and one hand. In the end I got old Jim to do it.

A few days later I got a reply. A crested envelope amongst the pile of bills, auction catalogues, agricultural ministry nonsense, and so on.

Dear Roger,
Thank you for your letter. It was good to meet up with you.
That is very disappointing, but I understand your concerns completely.
However I'm sure a way can be found to overcome those concerns, both to your advantage and to ours. This is a unique opportunity to benefit, not only both our own interests, but also those of the local community, the county, and indeed the economy as a whole. It is very rare that such a big opportunity comes one's way, and when it does one needs to think very carefully about the means to overcome all obstacles. There is always a way, given the right ingenuity and persistence.
Perhaps we might reflect a little longer, and then arrange another meeting. Either here in London or closer to home.
What do you say?'
Sincerely, George Collins.

His signature was like the swirl of a bramble thicket.

'Not going to give up easily, is he?' I said to Annie.

She was standing staring out of the window. That always meant she was pondering something. 'Well, are you sure we're doing the right thing?'

'Yes, I'm sure. Aren't you?'

She played with a strand of hair, which meant she wasn't. 'It's an awful lot of money.'

'We don't need money.' Well, not until the next farm crisis came

31

along, but I didn't say that.

'We're not exactly rolling in it.'

'Are you having second thoughts now?'

'Well, no but... I mean, he's right, we do need to give it thought.'

'We have thought.'

'Yes, but... two million pounds. And God knows what income from the toll charges. If they're prepared to offer so much money, they must be thinking there's a big business opportunity there.'

'That's what has me worried.'

'What?'

'Big businesses.'

'Well, it's the way of the world. You could... I mean, you could double the size of the farm. You could start whole new enterprises. There's no end to the opportunities it might open up.'

'Ah. You'd like me to become a tycoon like him.'

'No. But... well, thinking about it, I just think you need to think about it.'

'You got three thinks into that sentence.'

'Yes, so that's how much you need to think. It's an opportunity that would never come our way again.'

It was the other side of her that was talking now. The worldly side, the urbane side. It was something I was always up against, there lurking in the background.

She stopped twisting her hair. 'Have you told your dad about the deal?'

'Yes.'

'And?'

'He says it's up to me.'

'So he's not against it.'

I got angry then. My emotion against her logic. My primitive self against her mature self. My disability against her wholeness. I snapped, 'It's not him that will have to live with it, is it?'

She held up her hands and withdrew. She knew when to back off. I said I had to go and check on the caid lambs, and went out. I didn't want a row. I realised she was just working out her own thoughts, but

32

even so, it could turn into a fight quite quickly. She knew she was up against my rage with people, and I knew I was up against her calm.

Young Danny saw me heading for the lamb shed and hurried after. He always liked to go round the animals. He was sixteen and he'd have been a brilliant farmer if he'd been more mobile. He could walk a good distance, but he couldn't negotiate barriers, and he tired easily. But he was quite a help with the tasks he could manage. He could collect eggs and feed a caid lamb, but he couldn't shear a sheep or handle a young bullock. He had a strange brain. Slow at some things, genius at others. For instance he was no good at chess, but brilliant at blackjack. No one ever beat him at blackjack. He could memorise every card that had gone, and knew the odds on every hand. If we'd taken him to Las Vegas we'd have cleaned up.

We entered the lamb shed together. There were three or four orphan lambs in the pens, that we were trying to get together with surrogate dams. They needed regular checking to see how they were doing. If they didn't feed they could fade quickly. Old Jim usually checked them, but he was off doing something else, and anyway I needed to be out of the house.

Danny leant on the rail beside me to see into the lamb pen. His head just went over the top.

'Doing nice,' he said.

'Yep.'

'Jim let me give a bottle to that one.'

'Good. Did she take it?'

'Yeh. She's on the teat now.'

'Yes. That's good.'

We were quiet for a while, watching. I loved the smell in the sheep barn. The soft sound of rustling straw and the occasional lamb snicker. The house martins swooping in and out.

'We going to sell the farm?' Danny said.

'Lord no. Why d'you ask that?'

'What you were talking about. Putting a railway through.'

'Oh, we're not going to do that.'

'I went on the steam train at Keighley once with Grampa. I liked it.'

'Yes, that's fun. That's for tourists.'

He squinted at the ceiling, as he did when having big thoughts. 'Be quite fun having trains going by.'

'Not these ones. Great long freight trains trundling through, disturbing all the animals.'

'Hm.' Another pause. 'They want them for big stones?'

'Yes. Building blocks for all the houses and buildings going up everywhere.'

'Like the ones our house is built from?'

'Well, ours is granite, but a bit like that, yes. Only even bigger blocks.'

'They should float them down the river.'

'The river?'

'Yes. On big barges. I've seen them on the telly.'

'Well, yes, but you need a big wide river for that. Ours is too small and rocky.'

'Well then, they should build a canal. That's how they used to do it once.'

Not such a stupid idea. 'Well, the nearest canal is some way off. They'd have to dig another one to reach it. A lot harder than putting down rail tracks.'

'They could dig one along by our river. Wouldn't be as noisy as trains. And we could have a boat on it.'

I laughed. 'Trust you to think of a fun solution, Danny.'

'The thing is, you need lots of stones for a canal. So they could use their own stones.'

'Then they wouldn't have any left to build their buildings with.'

That shut him up for a while. But I could see him thinking it out.

I didn't answer the letter for several days. It sat on my desk glaring at me, like a poisonous mushroom. Then I got a phone call.

'Hello, Mr Oldfield.' It was the smart PA's voice. 'I have Mr Collins for you.'

I grabbed my coffee mug, slopping coffee on the mushroom.

He came on. 'Good morning, Roger. Just checking you got my letter.'

'Yes. Thank you. I wasn't sure how to answer it.' Meaning I didn't know how to do so politely.

'Well, how do you feel about another meeting?'

'Um... well, I don't think there's much point really. I won't change my mind.'

'Not even to discuss the money?'

'It's not the money, you see, Mr Collins. It doesn't matter if it was two billion. It's that the land is my life.'

There was a slight pause, then he spoke again. His voice had changed slightly. 'I think you need to reconsider, Roger. After all, we don't want to go down the route of local authority powers and compulsory purchase orders. That would open up a whole can of worms, wouldn't it? That would get us into new territory altogether.'

My turn to pause. The coffee had burned my mouth. 'You'd go that far?'

'This is a big project for us, Roger.'

I couldn't think of anything to say.

He let it run, then said, 'I think we should have that meeting. Why don't I come to you this time? Then we can discuss the whole thing whilst on the actual spot. Let the dog see the rabbit, as it were.'

Was I the rabbit? I knew I'd be no match for him when it came to business. But then he'd be no match for me when it came to shearing sheep.

I said, 'Er... well, do you really want to come all this way?'

'I think so. Much better have jaw, jaw, not war, war – as Churchill would have said.'

Oh well, once you've quoted Churchill there's no way out. So we arranged a date.

CHAPTER SIX

thirsday. 7.18. rainy nite. temp 18C. cows al down at river. mum doing

pan cakes for brekfist tiday my number 1 favrit. i wil finish my modil car

tiday. i mite change it to a steem engin. i think if evrybody went on trains

it wud be beter than going in cars. grampa says ther ar too meny cars but

i still lik cars. i wont dad to by a range rover 3 litre but he says its too

expensiv

Next morning, fine day - lambs were rap dancing and clouds scudding like race cars. I said to the family at breakfast, after I'd done the rounds, 'I'm going up to the top of Shere Fell. Who wants to come?'

'Me!' shouted Lily and Danny in unison, as I knew they would.

'What for?' asked my wife.

'I just want to get a view of their route,' I said.

'Won't tell you anything new. You've been up there lots.'

'No, but I want to get a birds-eye view. Everything looks different up there.'

'Well, I'll stay and do a clean while you're there. Mouse-eye view. Ready for you all to mess the house again.'

We left together – Danny and me in the buggy, Lily on her horse, Chardonnay, and Trigger running beside. It's quite a climb. Bumpy track, rocks and gullies, becks and peat quagmires. The whole history of the earth in that one giant hill. It's obvious why the ancients thought the gods lived in the mountains. I half believed it myself.

Danny loves going up, the buggy not so much. Shard and Trigger went the steep way, the buggy the zigzag way. Fast for the first half, slower on the next. Always a race, and either side could win. But we all got there, twenty minutes later panting and snorting.

You can see the whole world from up there. Well, half of

Yorkshire. Fold after fold of the Dales, surfing into the distance. Wide land and wider sky. Wind scything through everything except for the hawks free-riding the waves - sometimes just buzzards lazy spiraling, sometimes a peregrine lightning bolt, stooping from out of the sun. Despite them, rabbits everywhere. Occasionally a hare or a deer in summer. Sometimes a fox. Gorse and heather. Smells quite different to the valley. Heather and lemon, peat and pumice. Needles and pins.

We have a special rock where we sit. Wide and smooth as a hippo's bum, with views in all directions. I used to tell the children it was a piece of the moon that had fallen to earth, and they still almost believed it. You could live there for ever if you were tough as stone yourself.

We all four went to perch on it, with Chardonnay, pale gold as her name, grazing nearby. Danny had trouble climbing up, unlike Trigger. He puffed and grumbled.

'Not going to throw a tantrum are you, Danny?' I said, and held out my hand. 'Let me pull you.' He didn't like being helped, but he took hold and I heaved him up. We all sat together on the curving stone.

I took out my binoculars and studied the valley, sprawled far beneath like the model in the tycoon's office. You couldn't see the Stainbridge quarry from there, but I knew where it lay over the western fells.

I could also see part of Faulkner's farm, spread in the next valley over the hill's edge. Even from there it looked scruffy. Yes, it was obvious where the rail would have to run. Across the southern corner of his land between the two spurs of hillside, then curving round into our valley, following the line of the river on its way down to the Tees, like a silver snake in the grass.

'They'll have to cut through that wood,' I muttered to myself. 'And they'll have to cross that cleft in the hillside. Need a miniature viaduct to do that.'

'Let me see,' said Lily.

I handed her the binocs. 'Going to cost them a bomb,' I said.

She was peering. 'Be simpler to just bore a tunnel straight

underneath Shere Fell.'

'Yes, if money was no object. The Channel Tunnel cost squillions.'

Her green eyes gazed wide at me. 'What would we do with two million pounds?'

'That's their first offer. We'd probably get it up to three.'

'Okay, what would we do with three million pounds?'

'No idea. What would you do?'

Danny said, 'I'd put a steam train all round the farm, like the one at Keighley.'

'I think I'd start a stud farm, with the best stallions and mares one could find,' said Lily.

I nodded. 'Pretty good.'

'So what would you do?'

I thought. 'I'd probably build a new milking shed, new tractor, new hay baler, and then extend the ten-acre meadow to twenty acres.'

'That'd only take a bit of it,' she said.

'Well then, I'd get a helicopter so Mum and me could nip to York or London every week to go to the theatre.'

'Yes!' they both said in unison.

'But we're not going to do that, are we?' from Lily.

'No.'

We all watched the sky and the hills some more.

'That's a golden eagle,' said Danny. 'Or a vulture.'

'Don't think we have those in Yorkshire. Probably a buzzard.'

Lily was looking across the valley. 'You can see miles of dry-stone walls from here. All over the fells.'

They were another thing I loved. They were so old they were practically an organic part of the land. 'They say there's five thousand miles of them in Yorkshire alone.'

'And farmers really built them all?'

'Over hundreds of years. Cleared the ground and gave them sheep enclosures all in one go.' I had often wondered at it. The combined effort was probably as huge as three Hadrian's Walls.

'Lucky for us.'

'Yes. Tough doing. Takes a day to do five yards. Ten tons of stone.

Not a job I'd want.'

'I could do it,' said Danny. 'I can do jigsaws.'

'Yes, Danny, you could do it.'

Lily was solemn. 'Imagine spending your whole life building walls.'

'Some spend their lives doing that now. With bricks.'

'Some spend their lives *making* bricks,' said Danny. 'Or ice cream.'

You could hear a cow mooing from way down in the valley, and a shrike whistled from the river bank. The sky smothered us.

'There's Jim,' said Lily, pointing.

We could see him, way below, heading for one of the cow pastures. You could tell his bandy-legged walk even from here. I didn't know what his errand was, but I knew it would be something useful. Jim had been with the farm since early in my father's time. Nobody knew exactly how old he was. I don't think he knew himself. He lived with his equally old wife, Doris, in the small cottage at the far end of the drive. They looked like a pair of miniature matchstick people, skinny, wizened, as if someone had lit the matchsticks and let them burn a few seconds before blowing them out. They didn't weigh much more than matchsticks either. But Doris had acted as nanny to the kids when they were small, and she'd handled Danny then better than anyone – even Annie. And there was nothing Jim didn't know about farming - our farm in particular. He and I ran the whole shebang together, except for getting in extra help for the harvests, and lambing and shearing seasons. We didn't have anyone extra at this moment, so it was all hands on deck, even though the hands were odd numbers.

'Jim's spent all his life doing farm jobs,' Lily said. 'Not much different to walls really.'

I glanced at her. 'What are you going to spend your life doing?'

She was quiet. 'Dunno.'

'You could breed horses on the farm.'

'Not while you've got the cows though.'

'No, but... in the future.'

Danny said, 'Could I help?'

'Oh, yes,' she said. 'You could be my logistics manager.'

'What's that?'

'Someone who keeps the records of all the horses. All their details. Their height, their health, their training – all that.'

He nodded, satisfied. 'I could do that.'

'Probably make more than the cows,' I said. 'If you train good ones.'

'Yeh. More than the sheep even.'

A pair of grouse machine-gunned up from the heather nearby, and skimmed wide over the hill slope. Trigger barked and stood, quivering.

'Stay, boy,' I said.

We watched them disappearing across the fell's crest, fighter planes against the pale sky.

'It's the problem, isn't it?' I said. 'All this versus the modern world. How do you keep both?'

'Too many people, that's the trouble,' said Lily. 'We need to kill some of them off.'

'Woa! Who do you kill?'

'Well, at least stop them having so many babies.'

'China tried that. So everyone had only boy babies. Now the grownup boys have no one to marry.'

'Well, there you are,' she said. 'No marriages, no more babies. Problem solved.'

I laughed. 'Pretty drastic solution.'

'Pretty drastic problem.'

'I'd send lots of people to Mars,' chipped in Danny.

'It may come to that,' I said. 'But there's no grass or rivers on Mars.'

'I'd dig some, grow some.'

'Good.'

'And I'd have trains there.'

'Excellent.'

We stayed up there almost to lunchtime.

CHAPTER SEVEN

fryday. 6.26. windy nite. 14C. don't like big wind. i lisen to my mendelsun vilin when its windy. i can see the deer on the fel with my binocs. he only cums wen its erly or windy. i cal him damis becos the romans caled him that they use to liv heer. grampa ses the romans probly mad owr farm bicos they wer good farmers. they wer heer 2 thowsand yeers ago. he ses the farm wos probly lik owrs then. i lik that. i wil look for roman bones on the hil

They arrived on the dot. Trigger's bark warned us, and I could see them coming way down our long drive, past the peeling white fencing, the dirty pond with its ducks and moorhens, and the cow pastures on that side. The same big limmo, Harry the chauffeur, and three of them in the back. Father, son, and the other older man I'd caught trespassing.

I told Annie to wait in the house - although I knew she'd be peeking, along with my father - and met them in the farmyard. We shook hands as they got out.

'This is James Garrick,' said older Collins. His suit was a shiny film of opulence. 'Our project manager. He's the genius who has to work out all the technicalities, the costs, the timescales, and so forth. Much more important than either of us really.'

Garrick shook hands. His suit was more ordinary.

'So – done your walking holiday yet?' I asked. He gave me a sheepish smile.

'Well, you've had a long drive,' I said to them all. 'Would you like some tea, or a drink, or something.'

Collins looked at his watch. 'It's well into the afternoon. Why don't we wander down to the river and see the lie of the land? Then we can come back and chat over a glass of something.'

They'd come all that way. I could hardly refuse.

He reached back into the car and brought out a boxed bottle of whiskey. 'We've brought you a little gift. Malt whiskey. I'm sure you drink it sometimes.'

'Thank you, that's kind' I said, putting it on the doorstep. Then I looked at their feet. Smart city shoes. It had rained in the night. 'It's a bit muddy down there. I'd better lend you some boots.'

That threw them. 'Ah. Do you have some?'

'Oh, we always have boots for visitors. Come to the barn.'

The chauffeur stayed with the car. I led the way, and fixed them up with gum-boots from the row stuck on pegs on the wall. Pretty ancient most of them, mud and cow-dung stained, which contrasted nicely with their suits.

I called Trigger, and we walked five minutes down the track to the river. I didn't say anything on the way, just let them take in the scenery. We stood on the river bank, beside our single weeping willow. The cows gave us a glance, then went back to their grazing. The water grumbled over the rocks, only a few yards across at that point. Swifts skimmed the calmer pool further up. The place was putting on a good show.

'Good fishing, is there?' asked the son.

'There's trout and perch. We have had salmon lower down, but not often. I used to fish, but not so much now. Too busy.'

They nodded wisely.

Father Collins glanced upstream. 'Can we go and stand on the bridge? We'd get a good view from there.'

'Sure.' We walked along the farm track to the bridge, and stood on its humped summit, leaning against the stone parapet. The lower pastures stretched around us. The fells loomed on both sides, cloud shadows racing across their flanks. The water was quieter there.

They looked around for several moments.

'So what do you think, James?' asked the boss man. 'Feasible?'

The project manager was grunting as he studied the ground on the far side. He must have already known the answer. 'Yes, yes, not difficult. Fairly even levels. You'd hardly know it was there.'

'And as I said, we'd build you a bridge across where the culvert would cut through that mound over there,' said Collins. 'And as many level crossings for your animals as you wanted.'

'Wouldn't want the herd mown down by a monster train,' I said.

He laughed. 'Lord no! You'd have precise timetables. Couple of times a week, that's all.'

'There's quite a big cleft in the slope up at the far end. How would you get over that?'

Garrick said, 'Ah well, we'd build a small viaduct over that. Only needs a couple of hundred yards. Not too difficult.' He'd probably worked it out to the nearest stone.

'Let's walk the route,' George Collins said. 'Look at the problems close up.'

The four of us and Trigger crossed the bridge and walked along the other bank. I was looking for obstacles, but I had to admit there weren't many. Not until you got to the head of the valley where the hillside intruded closer to the river - a whale nosing onto a beach.

'We'd have to come quite close to the river bank here,' said the man. 'But it's out of sight of the house. Not much problem.'

Not for them maybe. A problem for the kingfishers and the family of water voles that lived in the bank there. 'Only a single track, you said?' I asked.

Collins nodded. 'With only a few trains a week, that's all we'd need. We'd run the empty wagons back on the same line.'

I pointed. 'What about the rest of the route beyond us?'

'It's council land and Forestry Commission. Not a problem.'

'Why don't you go west from the quarry instead, to Lancashire?'

'Too many hills, too many properties.'

They'd covered everything. 'So I'm your only problem? Me and the Faulkners.'

He half smiled. 'As I said, the Faulkners aren't a problem. So it's really just you.'

We made a pretence of studying the terrain for a bit longer, then

43

walked back to the house. They divested themselves of the boots, with much grunting and grimacing, then I sent Trigger to his kennel, and we went inside. I introduced them to Annie in the kitchen. I wasn't going to give them the honour of the drawing room. Lily was still at school, and it was one of Danny's special school days too, so the place was quiet. My father stayed out of the way.

Annie was giving them her charming sophisticated hostess act, but I knew she was nervous underneath. She was different when meeting town people. They were her own kind, the sort she was brought up with, but she became more coy, more self-conscious. In this case, the Collins's had a double effect on her, although I couldn't tell which affected her more, the urbane charm of the father, or the good looks of the son. Either way, she provoked stupid feelings in me.

It was snug in there. We kept the Aga going most of the time. Two of the cats rubbed around their legs. We all sat around the table, with much scraping of chairs on the ancient flagstones, and I opened their bottle. Expensive stuff. I poured us all a tot in our kitchen glasses.

Old man Collins sipped his glass, then said, 'Well, Roger, have you thought any more about our project?'

I liked the way he called it 'our project'. As if we were part of the whole business. As if it was a joint idea.

'Yes, Annie and I have talked it over at length. And Lily too of course. But I'm afraid we're still of the same opinion.'

He paused thoughtfully, then looked at Annie. 'What do you think, Mrs Oldfield?'

She gave him her Professor's daughter smile. 'Annie, please.'

'Annie.'

'Well of course, I'm with my husband. As he said, we've discussed it.' Her gaze flickered between him and the son. 'A railway through this valley just wouldn't be appropriate.'

I continued, 'I'm sorry you've come all this way, but I did warn you. We really don't want it.'

'Not even if we could improve the offer a bit?'

'Not even if you doubled it.'

They all three sat back in their chairs, with sombre faces. They looked like a trio of oligarchs who'd stumbled into the servants' quarters by mistake. The son had hardly spoken since they arrived. He glanced at his father.

The latter scratched his rugby jaw. Eventually he spoke. 'Well, Roger, that really does give us a bit of a problem. You see, this thing is too far advanced now for us to go back on it. We've got the local council involved, various government ministries, grant bodies, banks. We've got potential contracts with construction firms and council planners. This is a juggernaut that is going to take some stopping.'

I stared back at him. 'Don't you think you should have talked to us before you went to all that trouble?'

He smiled - the smile of a lord to a serf. 'Well, yes perhaps. But you see, we needed to find out if the whole thing was feasible before we approached you. We didn't think it would be a problem once you knew the size of the project, and the benefit to yourselves.'

'I'm afraid it is.'

'Hm.' He tapped his fingers on the table. They echoed the grandfather clock ticking in the hallway.

The son spoke up. 'Forgive me, but I... I don't quite understand why.'

I looked at him. 'Why it's a problem?'

'Yes. I mean, I understand why you're so attached to your lovely farm. And I was so impressed with all you told us about the importance of sheep to Britain's history, and all that...' He waved a hand on which a signet ring glinted. 'But, as we've explained, this would be of minimal impact to everything here, and would bring enormous financial benefit to yourselves.'

I glanced at Annie. She was listening to him intently. One of the cats jumped up onto the table top. I brushed it off with my arm.

'Minimal impact, you say.' I thought for a moment, looking into the depths of my glass. History floated there. 'Well, let me put it like this. If you had – let's say – a Van Gogh painting. Worth millions of pounds. And someone paid you to gouge a tear through it from top to bottom. Then it wouldn't be nearly so wonderful, would it? And it wouldn't be worth nearly so much.'

45

Silence. That stumped them.

'So, you're comparing your farm to a Van Gogh painting?' said elder Collins eventually.

'Yes. Not worth millions of course. But still...'

He nodded, a slow rock of the head up and down, staring at the tabletop. 'Right. Well, we'll have to think what to do next.' He looked up. 'Thank you for seeing us anyway. I don't think there's much point us talking further. We'll head back to our hotel now. We're staying in York.'

'Oh,' said Annie. 'I grew up there.'

Younger Collins smiled at her and said, 'Fine city.' She smiled back.

They got up, with more scraping of chairs. The goodbyes were polite - tight smiles and hand shaking. We waved at their rear window as they drove off.

'Whew! That was awkward,' said Annie.

'I told you they were smart people,' I said, watching her.

'A bit too smart. Coming all this way to pressurise us.'

I put an arm round her waist. 'Well, it's their loss. They wouldn't take no for an answer.'

'I hope they still won't.'

She was quiet that afternoon. I noticed, but didn't say anything. I had a hay field to mow.

CHAPTER EIGHT

toosday. 8.46. nice day. 25C. lily sed sum men cam yestiday wen i was at scool to see the farm. they cam in a big car i said wot kind but she didn no. dad had his sad look on wen i cum bac from scool. i don like his sad look. mum is sad too but she pritends not. praps the men told them sumthin rong.

Was I being stupid? Was I just being pig-headed? Was ideology blinding reality?

I asked Annie as we lay in bed that night. The wind had reared up in the evening, and it was moaning round the eaves like a pack of wolves. Perhaps an omen.

She thought for a long time, as so often, before she answered. 'It's tempting, but I know why you're against it. You must do what you think is right.'

I pulled the cover up further around us. It was a heavy patchwork quilt, half a century old, made by my grandmother. It smelt of musk and wool and probably a thousand copulations.

I said, 'When my grandfather got ill and knew he hadn't much time left, he made me sit by his bed - this bed - and he gripped my hand. I was only a teenager, but he said that I would inherit the farm one day, and that I had to preserve it. It wasn't just a matter of preserving the family legacy, he said. It was much more than that. It was a matter of preserving Britain. Britain had survived the Romans, the Vikings, the Normans, civil war, two world wars, Brexit, pandemics, and much else besides, and it had come through them all. Britain had given the world modern democracy and the rule of law. Britain, despite all, was as close to a civilised cosmopolitan nation as existed, whilst most of the rest were still in a medieval state. That's why we are headed by the most famous family on the planet. Why we've never succumbed to dictators.' The windows rattled and the curtains billowed with another blast of the wind. It brought the smell of animals. 'And, he said, it all goes back to its land. The land and Magna Carta. Only a small island, but it had the most diverse, beautiful, and productive land anywhere. It was the land that had fashioned the people. Fashioned the culture, the literature, the art, the character. Lose the land and you lose everything. You lose your identity.'

She smiled sleepily. 'Yes, I understand that.' She was used to my homilies.

I stroked her flank as she lay beside me. Winter or summer, we always slept naked under the covers. 'And he warned me that it was under threat even then. Threat from an ever-growing population, ever developing infrastructure and urban spread. Threat from soulless modern automation and invention. Threat of being forgotten.'

'You must keep it.' She turned towards me. 'But be careful. These seem like dangerous people.'

She was forgetting. I could be dangerous myself.

We heard nothing for weeks. I was beginning to think they had given up on us. The summer drifted by. A good summer. Enough rain to keep the pastures growing, not enough to flood the place. The trees flaunted themselves like dancing girls in French night clubs, and the hills sun-bathed like naked girls on French beaches. The price of lamb was high, and we did well at the auctions. The cows kept milking, the hens laying, the river flowing. Of course everyone loved the summer. Even though they knew they had to have the winter to remind them how good the summer was.

Then in late July a thick envelope arrived. It was marked Department for Transport. Inside was an official letter headed, 'Notification of Application for Compulsory Purchase Order'. Followed by a lot of bureaucrat's tranquilising jargon under a plethora of headings, APPLICANTS, OUTLINE, PURPOSES, LOCATION, PLANS, ENVIRONMENT, COSTS, TIMESCALE, APPEALS....

I stared at it for a long time. The longer I looked, the less it changed its message. Then I noticed another envelope. From the North Yorkshire County Council this time. Inside was a letter from the highways department requesting a surveyor's inspection the following Tuesday. The enemy had commenced action.

I had pushed it all to the back of my mind, hoping it would fade away, but here it was, rearing up again. I felt the engulfing shock of the threat, like being hit by an unexpected tsunami. It reminded me of the shock all that time ago – the shock a new enemy assault brought, just when you thought they had given up and drifted off into the mountains. Challenges rarely disappear. They just bide their time, waiting for the right moment.

Annie entered the kitchen with a basket of washing. Always one of the biggest jobs on a farm. If you want clean white shirts, don't be a farmer. She saw me sitting at the table.

'What is it?'

I handed her the first letter. She put down the basket and looked at it. She took more care over it than I did. I wasn't interested in the detail, only the bottom line.

Finally she said. 'So, is that it? Does that mean it's over?'

'No. It means it's just beginning.'

She threw me one of her looks. She knew about me and battles. 'You can't fight the government.'

'Who says? This is just the opening salvo. This is to find out whether there's any opposition. This is a sprat to catch a mackerel.'

'Hell of a sprat.' She started folding the laundry.

I had to admit it was a large one. Bulldozers coming, metaphorically and factually. 'They're sending surveyors to make an inspection next week.'

'Inspection?'

'Check it's all feasible.'

'Well, it is, isn't it?'

I nodded. 'Oh yes, it's feasible all right.'

I may have been up for battles, but I was at a loss when it came to red tape. 'I think we need some advice over this,' I said. 'I need to talk to Frank Carter.'

Carter was estate manager for Sir Peter Coverley, owner of an estate a few miles north. It was one of the county's finest, handed down since Henry VIII, several thousand acres of greenery. Mostly prime pasture. They'd had various brushes with the planning authorities in the past. Headed off an attempt to put a road through part of the estate, and stopped the building of a service station on one of the bypasses. And the baronet had been High Sheriff of the county. They'd know what to do.

I knew the manager quite well. We often met up at the sheep auctions. Loud raucous affairs, those were. All the farmers from miles around meeting up, buying and selling stock, fighting over prices, getting semi-pissed in the pub after. And if you've ever seen a bunch letting their hair down after they've been cooped up for a month with nobody but their animals, then you'll know what a fair old riot they can make. Sir Peter himself would come along sometimes too. He was the full aristocratic breed – Eton and Cambridge and fruity voice – but he would mix with them all as if he was one of their pig men, and could down a pint with the best of them. He even bought some breeding sheep from me occasionally.

I phoned the manager up. 'Frank, I've got a bit of problem. Need your advice. Can I come and see you?'

He didn't ask questions. We made an appointment for the next day.

I took Danny with me in the jeep. It was specially fitted out so I could drive it. One of those fine late summer mornings when the air was still and clear as crystal. Take a few deep breaths of it, and you're high for the rest of the day. On the way over the hills he talked incessantly as usual. This time about giraffes. He was obsessed with giraffes. Perhaps because they were so tall, and he was so short. He would go on about them for so long I was almost tempted to let him keep one in with the bullocks. I listened with half an ear. My mind was on other things. He only stopped when I drove up the long drive to the house.

The park, dotted with centuries old oaks, spread on either side,

Border Leicesters grazing peacefully under the crowded leaves. They had it easy compared to my tough old beasts on the hillsides. The house loomed ahead of me. Not the grandest of stately homes, but a big ancient pile even so. Limestone of course, and with that graceful sleepy air that said, 'I've seen so much history that nothing can surprise me.' It was the sort of place and the sort of family that the left despises. They'd have confiscated the land, hanged the baronet from the nearest tree, and turned the place into a refuge for the homeless if they could. They don't understand that much of the English countryside and traditions would be dead if it wasn't for such people. But then I'm old-fashioned.

I dropped Danny off at the box-hedge maze beside the formal garden. It was out of sight of the house, but in any case the family knew him and wouldn't mind. He knew the maze backwards. He had every turn memorised. He'd spend hours wandering its lanes.

Frank Carter was a gnarled Yorkshireman who'd been with his lordship for decades, and knew all there was to know about land and beasts. Knew how to live them, love them, and leave them. We met in the stable yard that was big enough to house an entire stud, and used to once upon a time. He took me into the tack room, where the smell of leather and horse and hay was enough to drug a prize fighter. He poured us both a whiskey from a leather-bound flask. The quiet sounds of munching, stomping, and snorting filled the background. Time ticked slowly around the oak beams.

'So what's up?' he said.

I told him the whole story.

He sipped his whiskey and pondered. His skin was the colour of the saddles around him, and his eyebrows could have been made of horse hairs. 'That's a tough 'un.'

'Yeh.'

'Ruddy railway line! Never met that one before.'

'No. Trains through the middle of the Dales. Hard to imagine.'

'For limestone, you say? Buildings?'

'Top quality apparently. They've got a lot of muscle behind them. County council, Ministry of Transport. Archbishop of Canterbury too, I shouldn't wonder.'

'Heh. What about environment? Protected areas?'

'They seem to have that covered.'

He sniffed and scratched his stubble. 'What does your old dad say?'

'Not much.'

His eyebrows twinkled. 'Never did say much. But I know what he'll be thinking.'

'Murder and mayhem.'

He chuckled. 'Aye. For sure the idea will have churned him up. As it would his dad's. But then they're an obsolete generation.'

'It churns me up too. Does that make me obsolete?'

He threw me a sympathetic look. 'No, Roger. No more than I am, or his lordship. But mebbe we're all fighting a losing battle.' He sighed, and twiddled a piece of straw, like a pen about to create an edict. 'Well, I think you could find enough objections to hold 'em up for a bit. You could cause them no end of aggro with appeals and reviews and all. Dunno if it'd stop them in the end though. Depends how determined they are.'

'They're determined.'

'And it'd cost a fair bit. Lawyers and surveyors and whatnot.'

'Mm.'

'What does that bugger Faulkner say?'

'I don't know what they've offered him. But I imagine he'll jump at it if it's two and sixpence.'

'Railway – bugger me! I'll have a word with the boss, and see what he says. He knows most of the people on the planning board. Maybe he can find out a bit more.'

'Thanks, I'd be grateful.'

He growled the growl of an ancient campaigner. The world is built on the shoulders of such. 'Anyways, we know the right legal and conservation people to go to. They owe us a favour or two.'

It's all about the people you know. In the end everything's about who you know. I always had to remind myself of that, because it was people I avoided getting to know.

I felt better. We drank a bit more whiskey, and chatted some more – about farming stuff, stock prices, what rubbish the English cricket team was, and so on – and then I left. I was none the wiser, but at least I had the comfort of some upper-class muscle at my back.

Danny was tired after going round the maze a dozen times. He slept all the way back.

CHAPTER NINE

tusday. 10.27. sun but rain cumin. 26C. yestiday went with dad to sur peters big hows i luv to go ther it has a big mase. i can dror the hole mase wen i get home. the gardin also has a lak and ducs and pee cocs and i saw a owzel wich is very rar. dad mor hapy cuming home than going ther. he is always hapy after he talks to frends. i wish i had mor frends. mi best frends ar lily and jim and jo taxy man. lily has lots of frends at scool but i dont. mum ses lam for diner to nite and jam pud mi number 1 favrit. mite do my colecshins tiday

We shouldn't have worried. The gods took a hand in the whole business.

Two days later it started to rain. I was coming back from the fields with Trigger, when it came on heavy, as only August rain can. I went into the hay barn, and sat on a bale. Trigger squatted beside me. The rain battered on the corrugated roof like the gods knocking to come in. I loved that sound. One of the cats sheltering there brought us a dead mouse. I said thank you, and stroked the purring tabby.

But three days after that it was still raining. Rain such as you only get in the Dales. Rain drops the size of cannon balls. And winds blowing them across the meadows as fast as cannon balls. I knew now that this was serious. We had basked in too good a summer for too long. I should have known from experience – the weather never lets you breathe for long. It's always a sleeping giant.

The farmyard was swimming. The barns were swimming. The animals were knee deep in water, huddled together wherever they could find shelter. The fields were sodden quagmires. The trees wilted under the assault like sailors under the lash. The streams were marauding torrents charging down the fellsides. And the river got fuller and fuller.

In the middle of the third night it burst its banks. We woke in the morning to find the whole base of the valley under water. Of course we'd had floods before, but none on this scale for decades. The livestock were safe. We had moved the cattle up onto the high pasture, and the chickens and domestic creatures to dry places. But the farm itself and the outbuildings, raised a little above the valley floor, were marooned in a lake that stretched right to the base of the hills. We were an island in an uncharted ocean.

I took photos from the bedroom window. Then I waded out towards the river as far as I could and took more photos. Wild creatures were desperately swimming around seeking a landing place. Small corpses floated by, dead leaves on the flood. With the long lens I got the river bridge just showing its parapets above the flood. A larger beast swam by - badger, wild cat, I couldn't tell. I felt as though I was drowning too. My world was under water.

However, the rail route was under water too.

I emailed all the photos to the Collins's secretary with the terse message, 'Here's another obstacle.' I got no reply.

We were trapped for almost a week. I could just get through the floods in the jeep, but there wasn't much point - the whole area was semi-submerged. I wished we had a sailing boat. It was a week of impotent tedium. We played games, we watched television, we dawdled on the internet. Lily and myself suffered the worst. She, prevented from getting to school and from riding Shard. Me from doing anything meaningful at all. Danny was best off. He had innumerable ways of entertaining himself – on his laptop, with his diary and his scribblings, his weather statistics, or watching from the upstairs windows with his binoculars. Annie spent her time bottling and baking stuff, and re-reading her favourite books.

However, the one light in the darkness was that this would surely scotch the rail plans.

Gradually the rain clouds drifted off towards the Channel, and the waters subsided enough for us to venture out again, and survey the damage. Beaten fields, damaged fences, blocked ditches, debris everywhere. Ravaged nature. At least most of the sheep had stayed safe, sodden and weighed down, but above it all, stoic as ever. And we could start to move the cattle around the driest parts. But the wreckage was a dispiriting sight. It would take weeks to repair everything.

Nevertheless, through all the sodden misery and death, through the elemental flexing of cosmic muscles, I felt a strange composure. It was just another of nature's challenges. We had come through them before, and we would again. It was all part of the game.

The council inspectors of course had put off their visit. I assumed they wouldn't bother to come now. But some days after the floods had receded, I received a phone call.

'Sorry, we couldn't keep the appointment the other day,' said the brusque Yorkshire voice. 'Would it be convenient for us to come tomorrow?'

I frowned. 'Er... is there much point? The rail route was way under water. The company surely aren't going to continue with their plans?'

'Ah, well sir, that's not really our concern. We still have our instructions, so we need to come and take a look.'

I reluctantly agreed a time the next afternoon. They arrived twenty minutes late, having lost their way. I had experience of their species. Usually failed architects and surveyors who'd got jobs with the council that no one else wanted, and were now little dictators who loved throwing their weight around just because they had the power. This pair were a small tubby man with a bald head and a dismal expression, and a gawky younger fellow who was probably a trainee. Their car wasn't nearly as smart as the Collins's, and neither were their suits. They may have been late, but they were loaded with notebooks and plans and ordnance survey maps and laser distance measurers – possibly grass blade counters for all I knew.

The farm had superficially returned to normal by now. I took them on the same tour all over again, and listened to them making the same comments. Then we came back to the yard. I didn't ask them in.

The older man made a big show of writing notes on some form or other, then said, 'Well, Mr Oldfield, we'll be putting our report in to the council, and no doubt you'll be hearing back.' An air of bureaucratic smugness hung about him like body odour.

'Is it the council who'll be dealing with it?'

'No. It's too big for that. We're just doing the report. This will go to Whitehall – the minister.'

'So – apart from it being under water every so often - you think there are no obstacles to a rail line through our farm?'

He lifted his chin at me. He was a good six inches shorter. 'No practical obstacles that we can see. And as for the floods, that may not be too much of a problem.'

'What? Why?'

He waved a hand towards the distant quarry. 'It would be entering your valley at a height, so they'd build an embankment anyway across the low-lying parts.'

I stared. 'An embankment?'

'Just a couple of metres high. But enough to raise it above any real flood threat.'

My brain did a somersault. 'They said the line would hardly be noticeable.'

He smirked. The smirk of a man who was paid by the taxpayer and only cared about his retirement pot. 'Ah well, it depends what you mean by noticeable. You'd come to see it as just part of the landscape anyway.'

'No, we wouldn't.'

He shrugged, chewed his pudgy lip, and said nothing.

I said, 'What about environmental factors?'

'Well, that's not really our concern.'

'Seriously? Then whose concern is it?'

'Um, well... depends on what sort of appeals anyone might make. What local objections, and so on.' His piggy eyes squinted at me. 'Do you think there may be some?'

'Oh yes, there'll be objections all right.'

'Yes, well... there usually are. They need to be sent in using the procedures in your notification. They'll be considered by the relevant departments.' He looked disappointed, as if he wished it was him doing the considering. He scanned the yard, metaphorically wrinkling his nose at the sodden farm smell. 'We'll leave you to it then.'

They got into their car and drove off. The younger one had barely said three words. I stood staring after them for a long frozen moment. I wondered whether a bomb under the council offices might be feasible.

The next day I got another phone call. I hated hearing that phone ring, but this time it was a good call.

'Mr Oldfield? My name's Jeremy Driscoll. Sir Peter Coverley suggested I get in touch.' It was another of those well-educated city voices, moulded to give confidence. 'I gather you have a bit of a problem with a compulsory purchase order.'

'Yes, that's right.' I glanced at Annie, who was doing the mail at the desk. It was funny, but opening envelopes was one of the few things I found hard to do. She was watching with her eyebrows raised. She could hear most of what was said.

'Well, I'm a lawyer specialising in that sort of thing. Land acquisition, environment issues – all that stuff. I've done quite a bit of work for Sir Peter in the past.'

'You're local?'

A chuckle. 'No, no, I'm based in London. But we do work everywhere.'

'Ah. Did Sir Peter tell you what it was about?'

'Yes, he did. And in fact I've had a look at the application. Interesting case.'

'You've already seen it?'

'Yes. Once issued, it's publicly available.'

Wow, I thought, these people don't waste time. 'So what do you think?'

'Oh, shouldn't be too much of a problem. I think we can scotch this one pretty smartly.'

'Really?'

'Oh, yes.'

A huge weight that I hadn't realised was there seemed to lift from my shoulders. 'But won't it entail hearings and appeals and so on. Won't it be expensive?'

'Oh, I doubt it will get that far. We'll let them all know there are going to be appeals to the Lands Tribunal. Then all we have to do is supply the opposition with our list of objections, and once they realise they won't have a leg to stand on they'll probably drop the whole idea.'

'What objections?'

'Ah, you leave that to me. They won't know what's hit them. Practical issues, legal issues, environmental issues, precedent issues...'

'Precedent?'

'Yes. This could be opening up all sorts of precedents. Potential mining exploration all over the protected areas. Vast quarries dug into the hillsides. Railway lines running everywhere – worse than Clapham Junction. I'll make it seem like Armageddon. We'd have the whole county up in arms.'

'Right.' I was too overwhelmed to think straight. Annie was listening with eyes shining. 'So, um... do you want me to come to London to see you?'

'No, that won't be necessary. I've got all the details of the plan. I've got Google maps to show me what is where. I'll send you an outline of our charges, and if you're happy I'll prepare a list of our proposed objections. Scare the pants off them.'

'Simple as that?'

'Well, they're evidently a big outfit. No doubt they'll spend some time trying to find a way round it. But in the end I'm confident they'll realise it's a waste of time.'

'Well, that's great.'

'The only caveat is that they might then try to put pressure on you to drop your objections before it got to court. How well do you know them? How ruthless are they?'

'I don't know. They're pretty determined.'

'And how determined are you?'

'Very.'

'Right. Well, we'll cross that bridge when we come to it.'

If he'd been in the room I'd have kissed him. I went and kissed Annie instead.

The vet came on a visit that afternoon. A couple of the Shorthorns with problems after the flood – nothing too serious, but I always liked to have them checked. Fred Hordern was near seventy years old, been around the Dales all his life, knew every farmer for miles – every field, every beast, every grasshopper probably. He was hugely overweight, with crumbling knees, dodgy heart, and drank like a giant squid, but he loved his job. If you asked him why he didn't retire, he'd say either the boredom would kill him, or his missus would. Anyway I was always glad to see him.

Old Jim and I went with him to the field. Danny came too of course – ever intrigued when the vet came. The four of us checked the two cows, the vet examining their mouths, feeling their udders.

'What d'you think, Danny?' asked Big Fred.

'Mastitis, I reckon,' said Danny.

Fred winked at me. 'He'll be pinching my job soon.'

Jim just nodded. He rarely said much.

The vet gave me some stuff for them. Then he checked Trigger, who was limping, and treated a sore in his paw. The he checked me, said I looked fine, and we went inside for our customary noggin. I sent Danny off with Jim to do an early egg round, poured Fred some of the Collins's malt whiskey, and told him the story.

He listened to it all, took another swig of the whiskey, smacked his lips at it, and said in his broad Yorkshire accent, 'Ayup, that'd cause a right rumpus around the county. Railway through the fells? The lads won't be likin' that.'

'The march of progress, they call it in London.'

'Ay well, bugger progress. They'll be getting another kind of march if they push this through.'

'You think so? You think the locals would rally?'

'Oh ay, you bet. Spread the word, we'd have half of Yorkshire up in arms. We'd have Oliver Cromwell up from his grave.'

Annie came into the kitchen, rubbing cream on her hands. 'Hello, Fred. Saw your car outside.' He struggled to rise, but she pushed his big weight back in the chair. The chair complained. 'Don't get up. That bottle's strong stuff.'

'Yer lookin' gorgeous as ever, Annie,' he said.

'Flatterer.'

'I'm straight. I'd chase you round the table if I could get up.'

She laughed. 'I'm nearly forty.'

'So what? A woman isn't ripe till she's forty.'

'You're a dirty old man.'

'Aye. Gettin' dirtier and older every day. Roger here's bin tellin' me yer train problem.'

'Yes.' She went to put the kettle on. Not one for alcohol in the afternoon, Annie.

He watched her. 'What are you thinkin'?'

She stopped, iron kettle hovering above the Aga. We had an electric one, but she rarely used it. 'Me?'

He squinted, beady-eyed. Didn't miss much, the vet. 'Offered a lot of money, I gather. Are you tempted?'

She threw me a glance. 'We've discussed it. Yes, it's tempting. But it could open the floodgates, couldn't it?'

'Ay, it could that. Question is, what would you do if you had the money?'

'I don't know. The question doesn't arise. We've decided.'

'There's lots would take it.' Including him, I thought, but maybe not.

She turned by the stove, eyes smiling. 'Are you trying to entice us, Fred?'

His fat cheeks inflated. 'No, no, not at all. Just prodding.'

'Save your prodding for your animals.'

He nodded and held out his glass for a refill. By the time he left the bottle was empty.

When I came back from seeing him off, Annie was still standing by the stove, tea-cup in hand, staring at the floor. I knew that look.

'What is it?'

She raised her head. A hair strand fell over her face. 'I still think we should consider their offer. That lawyer asked how ruthless they are. Why would he ask that?'

I shrugged. 'I dunno. Just being cautious.'

'We don't want any more worry, Roger. We've had enough stress.' With Annie, stress was like a hot iron on the skin. With me, it was more like nagging indigestion.

'You don't think a railway would bring stress?'

'Well, I...' She brushed the hair away and sipped her tea. 'A different kind of stress perhaps. But we'd get used to it. I mean, would it make that much difference? I mean *real* difference?'

'Yes.'

'In what way?'

I considered. What could I say that would strike a chord with her? 'It would be like having an enormous discord erupting right in the middle of your favourite Mozart concerto. Every time you listened to it.'

She was quiet for a second. Then she burst out laughing. 'You are a bugger! Trust you to find an argument.'

Yes, well finding neat musical metaphors was one thing. Keeping the whole orchestra in tune was quite another. The stress was on a high note. The buildings hummed with it.

CHAPTER TEN

sun day. 6.51. rain gon. 21C. fred vet cam yestiday. we went to see the sic
cows. i mite be a vet 1 day. the fluds hav gon now they wer the wirst ever
they nirly coverd the brige and drownd lots of rabits and insecs. we moved
all the cows to the top feelds and got all the hens and ducs to the old barn
and got all the cats indors it was very ecsiting. i sed wos it god did it but
dad sed no it was nachur. i dont under stand why god dusnt tel nachur wot
to do. or peepl. mum cookd lots evry day but ran owt of pan cakes flowr.

It was my fault. I always felt it was my fault. Not my accident, but the other one.

Danny was one of twins. Then, still only embryos little more than six months old. His sister didn't survive it. Perhaps it was just as well. She'd have been even more brain damaged than he was.

Annie was twenty-eight weeks pregnant when it happened. I was taking her for a ride up the valley on the old buggy. I should have known it was a risky thing to do, but she was finding her confinement hard, and she so wanted to get out into the sunshine. Despite her yearning for the city, she had a great love of the outdoors.

Her favourite place on the river was at the far end of the land, where the bank was high and the waters tumbled over a sculpture park of rocks. She loved to sit above the swirling rapids and watch the wildlife darting about the currents and the rock slabs.

I drove the buggy over the usual route, along by the fields and past the beech wood as I had done a hundred times before. The only difficult part was where the track tilted as it approached the river bank. I always took that stretch slowly, especially when the ground was wet. This day was fine, but it had rained overnight and the earth was sodden and slippery. I shouldn't have risked it, I should never have risked it, as I told myself a thousand times afterwards. But I did, not thinking much about it. The buggy hit an especially sodden part, and started to slither towards the edge. I tried to brake, then to accelerate out of it, but there was nothing I could do. We went over the edge. The buggy fell onto its side, hurling us both out onto the sloping bank, and we tumbled for yards over the turf.

She lay there for minutes, eyes open, breathing deeply, not badly hurt, but knowing that something was happening inside her. The sunlight splintered her face, the river rumbled below. I managed to right the buggy, and to lift her onto it. I had two arms then. I got her back as quickly and as gently as I could, and then drove her in the car to the hospital at Barnard Castle. They delivered the twins there, twelve weeks prematurely. They managed to save Danny, but not his sister.

It was my fault. She never blamed me for it. She always insisted that it was just one of those things, but I knew it was my fault. It was one of those moments that, when you look back over your life, you wish you could just do over again. You wish it again and again.

Danny was the tiniest thing you ever saw. How he could be that small, and still living and breathing you couldn't imagine. But he grew and developed, and eventually started crying and kicking and feeding properly. The doctors had hopes for him, but when he was a few months old we knew that things weren't quite right. He was extremely advanced in some ways, and extremely backward in others. And as the months and years passed those traits grew. He found his own ways to cope with life. He developed his own unique personality, his own moods and methods. He was prone to great rages when the world refused to accommodate him as he wished, but also great pleasures when he managed to exploit the world to his design. He had huge frustrations and huge affections. Including his affections for us, and for all the animals on the farm – wild or domestic. He saw us all as part of the same. Part of his small universe.

We all brought him up. Annie and me and Lily and old Jim's wife, Doris. My parents too when they were both alive. They were almost as distressed as we were at what had happened. They had moved to the old dairyman's cottage when they got too old to run the farm, and left me to it. But they loved the kids, as grandparents do. My father especially, who had been pretty tough on me when I was young. He took to Danny like he was his own. The two of them would spend hours together making stuff and playing strange games. Whenever Danny got fed up with the rest of us he would wander down to the cottage to see them, and we knew he'd be gone until he got hungry for more than the biscuits my mum made. Now, he still went to see dad in the dairy flat when he was bored.

Everyone learnt his ways and his idiosyncrasies. He didn't distinguish between any of us. We were just the natural denizens of his world, along with Trigger and the cats and the birds and the farm beasts. It was a small horizon, but he was happy with it. He was lucky in a way.

It was for him as much as anyone that I needed to protect the land.

CHAPTER ELEVEN

sun day. 10.17 hot 28C. i mad a list of my favrit peeple in my book. it went

- 1 mumdad - 2 lily - 3 grampa - 4 jimdoris - 5 triger - 6 jo taxy man - 7

mis tomas teecher - 8 fred vet - 9 jon vilij shop — 10 cris milk truc. mum

red me new story last nite abowt sno wite and 7 dworfs. i think its a sily

story but i lik the 7 dworfs. i think im happy dworf or perhaps doc. and

sumtims grumpy. i like storys abowt reel peepl best. like i rite in my diry

Funny how things come in waves. Nothing happens for days, weeks at a time, then it all comes at once. Two days later we got yet another visit. We were popular people all of a sudden.

However this was an unpopular visitor. Brad Faulkner himself, our neighbouring farmer, clattering into the yard in his old utility, vomiting diesel fumes. I was in the tractor shed with Jim when he arrived. I left Jim to finish changing the oil on the Fordson, and came out to meet him, Trigger at my heels. He clambered out, broad, pot-bellied, half shaved, his habitual glowering expression darkening the day.

'Hello, Brad,' I said, wiping my hand on a rag so I wouldn't have to shake.

He looked around my now tidy yard as though it was a slag heap. 'We need to talk.' He had a voice like the Fordson warming up.

'Sure. Go ahead.' I wasn't going to invite him in either.

'Why are you objecting to this rail thing?'

'Why d'you think?'

'There's big money involved here.'

'There certainly is.'

His chin was jutting like the prow of an ice-breaker. 'So, why?'

I was silently conjecturing how simple life would be without

66

money. If we could go back to the days of bartering sheep and eggs. 'How much have they offered you?' I asked.

'That's my business. But they must have offered you more. Why are you turning them down?'

I sighed. 'Well, if you don't know, Brad, I can't explain it to you.'

His face went more flushed than it already was. He'd been drinking, and it was only eleven in the morning. 'Don't give me that airy-fairy stuff about protecting the environment. This is the world now. They're going to win one way or another.'

'Not if I have anything to do with it.'

'Course they will. You can't fight big business. You can't fight London.'

'I can try.'

A look of genuine puzzlement creased his face. Trigger's head bent sideways as if registering his bewilderment. 'I don't understand. You could give up farming. Give up trying to do this shitty work one-handed.'

'I like doing this shitty work.'

'But it'd make you a rich man. Why?'

'I don't need to be a rich man. I'm happy as it is.'

'You'd be a lot happier.'

'Not necessarily. Do you know a lot of happy rich people?'

'I don't know any rich people. But I'd bloody well like to be one of them.'

Dream on, my friend, I thought. A loud clanking came from Jim in the tractor shed. 'Well, I'm rich enough already, thank you.'

He sniffed, brushed his hand through his rook's nest hair, looked up at the sky as if for divine assistance, and folded his thick arms. 'Look, Oldfield, I need this deal. If you scotch it, you scotch mine too. They only want to cross part of my land, but what they're offering could save my entire farm. I'm in trouble there.'

I was in no mood to be sympathetic. 'Yes, well maybe if you farmed it a bit better you wouldn't be in trouble, Brad. We've talked about this.'

His tractor voice growled still further. 'Don't you lecture me about farming. I've had bad luck is all. Drought, disease, market prices... and now the bloody flood!'

'Has it caused you much damage?'

"Course it has! Turned my yard into a quagmire. Lost me several sheep.'

I could picture his drab farmstead. He wouldn't have taken enough precautions once the rain started. 'It's all part of farming, Brad. Dealing with the challenges.'

'Bugger the challenges!' He leaned back against his truck, contemplating the dirt on the ground for several seconds. Then his bleary eyes fired back. 'Well, look here, Oldfield – I don't intend to lose this deal. It's a lifeline for me, and for my family. You need to think very carefully before you turn it down.'

'Or what?'

'Or there'll be serious repercussions.'

'Are you threatening me?'

He glowered at the ground for another long moment. Then he half raised his head and stared from under thick brows, so that I could barely see the whites of his eyes. His right hand twitched as though holding a club. 'I've got two sons who are looking to inherit my farm, and I'm going to see they do.'

Knowing his sons, I didn't think that would mean any improvement. He'd had a wife too once, but she'd given up on him long ago. Everyone has redeeming features, but I hadn't yet discovered what his family's were.

I said, 'I'm glad you're thinking of your sons, Brad. I hope they'll farm it better than you do.'

He raised his head fully now, and his look would have curdled milk. 'You're an obstinate bastard, aren't you?'

'Yes.'

He climbed back into his utility. 'You'll be hearing from me.' And he drove off, almost assassinating a stray duck from the pond as he went.

It's a sad thing, but a lot of our so-called sophisticated species are anything but sophisticated. In fact a lot are just plain primitive.

Evolution has a way to go yet.

Old Jim came bow-legged out of the shed behind me. He'd been listening. He sniffed at the fumes from the truck, drowning all the farm smells.

'Right old bugger, that one.'

'Mm.'

'His sons are as bad.'

I looked at him. He was hardly one to mix with the family. 'Do you know them?'

'See them sometimes down the village. They drink at the Wheatsheaf.' This was the scruffier of the village's two pubs. I knew Jim went there sometimes at weekends. 'Always looking for a fight.'

'Well, they'd better not look for one here.'

'Ar. Better keep the shotgun loaded even so.' He went back to the tractor.

If I knew anything from farming, I knew one thing. You need to be prepared. You need to anticipate. Disasters can strike from anywhere, but if you're prepared then at least you have a chance at surviving them. Me, and my father, and his father had survived storms, droughts, disease, foot-and-mouth, market collapses, idiot regulations, you name it. I'd even survived my accident. We'd come through because we'd always kept one step ahead of the game. We'd built defences, kept reserves.

The question now was, what were my defences? It was hard to anticipate when you had no idea of what the danger might be, or which direction it would come from. I had a family of five, several hundred animals, and a thousand acres to safeguard. I felt like Horatius at the bridge.

Well, as Jim said, at least I could keep the shotgun loaded.

CHAPTER TWELVE

wednsday. 12.13. strata clowds. 22C. did droring leson with dad. i wonted

to dror girafs agin and cars but he wonted me to dror sumthin difrint. i had

a tan trum but then i did a reely good fordsun tracter like owrs and dad was

pleesd. the farmer next dor cam after in his ford truc and i cud see dad and

him havin argiment. dad gets his funy look on wen he has a argiment and

his stump wigils. the man fritins me he nirly kild a duc wen he went owt

I always knew when Annie was down. I could tell from the droop in her shoulders, the grey in her expression. Like a partial eclipse of the moon. As this particular morning. She put lunch on the table, but said little, and I saw she was feeling the strain.

I always felt a bit beholden to her. I had taken her away from the city - from her beloved galleries and bookshops and social life, and I knew that a part of her hankered for them. I tried to fill in the gaps, but there was ever a small void lurking in her soul. And a bigger void because of Danny and what had happened.

But I knew what to do. 'Tell you what,' I said. 'I'm taking a few ewes to the Barnard Castle sheep market tomorrow. Forecast's good. Why not come too?'

That did the trick. She lit up immediately. It wasn't much of a town, only twenty minutes away, but there were things there that lifted her spirit beyond cattle and sheep and railway lines. We'd have no objection from Danny, who loved walking castle walls. And I quite liked returning there. Apart from the market, it was where I'd been to school.

'Yes, let's do that. We can have lunch in the town.' She was cheerful for the rest of the day. Women's moods can turn on a sixpence. Men take longer.

Early next morning, before leaving, I was looking at the accounts, and she was making a few dozen loaves of bread in the kitchen, when the phone rang.

'Good morning, Roger. Martin Collins here.' Collins the younger. I was torn between perplexity and apprehension. 'I hope I'm not disturbing you. I'm actually in Yorkshire, heading for Northallerton to the council offices. Got a meeting there this morning. I wondered whether I might drive over and see you this afternoon? Nothing particular, just for a chat.' They get about, these Collins's.

'I think we've said all there is to say, Martin.'

'Well, yes, I'm fully aware of your views, but there might be... well, there are a few other things to consider, and um...'

'What sort of things?'

'Oh, just the general situation. I think it might be beneficial if I could see you briefly. Father's in London – it's just me. I'm driving.'

I pondered for a moment. Was this some kind of trap? Was he being sent as a messenger boy? I had no desire to play these devious games, but on the other hand it was an opportunity to find out what they were up to. 'Well, Annie and I are planning a trip to Barnard Castle today. Have you ever been there?'

'No. Can't say I have.'

'Oh, well you'd find it worthwhile. It's not far. Why don't you meet us there?'

'Er... well, all right. Is the castle easy to find?'

'Oh, yes. It's a town. Your satnav will find it. Let's say, by the castle tower at two o'clock. You can't miss it. How would that suit?'

'Yes, fine.' He sounded dubious, but he could hardly refuse.

I told Annie. Her expression was blank. I said, 'It might be a chance to discover more of what they're thinking. You and Danny can go off to the museum if you don't want to be in on it.'

That worked. The Bowes Museum was one of her favourite places. On the edge of town, and housed in a vast Victorian palace looking like a French chateau drunk on Nuits St Georges, it held enough old masters and exotic stuff to keep both her and Danny enthralled all day. One of those eccentric follies that the British aristocracy, with nothing better to do, have installed in odd places around the land over the centuries. She'd been there half a dozen times, but never tired of it.

'Yes,' she said. 'I don't want to talk trains any more.'

For once the weather forecast got it right. It was a fine day as we drove over the border and into Durham County through the hills. The countryside danced in the light shafts. You could see the ruins of the castle from miles way – shattered survivor of God knows how many battles and sieges – tottering above the Tees as if about to take its final plunge into oblivion.

We were cramped together in the cab of the jeep, with the sheep in the back. Old Jim had groused a bit when I said we'd be going. He always liked to do the market days, but he deferred to the family. I left him with the odious job of finishing the sheep dips.

I was going to drop Annie and Danny in the town centre, whilst I went on to the market. However, as we approached the town, she said, 'No. Take us straight to the museum now. We'll do that whilst you're selling your sheep, and then we can meet you for lunch, and come on with you to the meeting at the castle after.'

'I thought you didn't want to talk trains,' I said.

'I think I should be there.' She had her stubborn face on. 'I'd like to hear what he has to say.' I knew better than to argue. I'm the boss in our household, but I need her permission to say so.

I dropped them at the entrance to the huge Gothic museum, squatting like a benign ogre in the sunshine, and drove on to the market. I spent an hour there, in between the auction bids chatting to Big Fred the vet, and a couple of the local farmers. They'd all heard about the rail thing. They were keen to know what was happening, but I didn't say too much. Give a whisper in that community, and within minutes it's become scandal of the month.

The market was its habitual heaving, shouting, smelling circus. All of humanity exhibiting all of its quirks. The scene probably hadn't changed much for a thousand years. Prices were good. I sold the ewes for near the hundred mark apiece, and even got cash for a couple. But this time I wasn't staying for the usual lunchtime pub session with the farming folk. I walked back from the auction ground, to the familiar town streets with their ancient frontages, often dismally gaunt as only northern townships can be, but today glowing in the sun. The ghosts of visitors like Walter Scott, Dickens, and Turner loitered round every corner. The three of us had lunch in Danny's favourite café, where they did toasted sandwiches big enough to make a road block, and then we wandered up to the castle.

We were early, but that was fine. There were few other sightseers there. We walked the walls and climbed to the tower as we'd done a dozen times before, Danny puffing behind us. I could just see the roofs of the school where I'd baited teachers a quarter of a century ago. Bigger and smarter now, with facilities my generation never dreamed of, and charging an Arab tycoon's ransom in fees. Taught a few Arab tycoon's kids as well. Education was one of those things that had improved over the years, though I wasn't sure how much it showed.

Martin Collins arrived bang on time, dressed in tweeds this time – country outing. With him was a very pretty blonde, which I hadn't expected. She was all long hair and high heels and pricey fashion coat.

They came up to where we were sitting on the thousand year-old stones, and we shook hands. Annie had her flirty urban look on as he took hers. She was probably a decade older than him, but you wouldn't have known.

'This is my fiancée, Julia,' he said. 'I hope you don't mind. She came along for the trip. She's never been to Yorkshire.'

'It's beautiful,' she said. 'I never realised.' She had a nice smile, not too affected.

'No, well, you're actually in Durham now,' I said, 'but it's all part of the same. All the way up through Northumberland to the Scottish border. Countryside such as you never see down south.'

'No. It brings the Brontes to life.' So she read as well. That was good.

'This is our son, Danny,' I said, in the simple way I always introduced him. They didn't react to him – just shook hands as if to anyone else. He gave his lopsided grin, and immediately launched into the things he had seen in the museum that morning. Dates, provenance, history, the lot. They listened with quiet fascination.

Annie said finally, 'All right, Danny, that's enough. They don't want an entire inventory. Perhaps they'll go and see for themselves.'

'It sounds fascinating,' said the girl. 'We should certainly go.'

'So why did you want to meet again?' I asked Martin.

He frowned, and searched the sky as if seeking help there. 'I just... we still need some clarification as to your real objection to the scheme. My father feels there's something you're not telling us.' He waved a vague hand. 'You must understand his mentality. Of course he gets your aesthetic fears for the landscape, but as a businessman he can't comprehend why someone would turn down such a profitable opportunity.'

I too looked up at the sky. I was so tired of explaining to people. Then I glanced at Annie. She was no help. She was staring at him with an odd expression on her face. It wasn't like mine, one of frustration. It was more like intrigue. I felt a twinge of irritation at them both.

I turned back and said, 'Come on up to the viewpoint on the wall.' I led the way up the steps to where it overlooked the river gorge. From there you could see far over the farming land to the distant shapes of the Dales. 'See that?' I said. 'Look beyond the town sprawl, and you can barely see a building for fifty miles. Just farms and small villages that have hardly changed in two hundred years.' Cloud shadows chased across the fields. 'Smartened up a lot of course. Especially by wealthy people escaping the fug of the city.'

They looked for long moments. The river below swished its way over the rocks. Pure as diamonds until it reached the pollution of the eastern cities. What they were thinking I couldn't guess.

'The thing is, you see,' I said, closing my coat against the breeze up there, 'it's not just one little railway line. It's the gradual eating away over the years, that means you wake up one morning and realise you've lost it. Or your kids wake up and don't know they ever had it. They'll never know the deep thrill of nature, the peace of unspoilt landscapes, the satisfaction of nurturing the earth. They'll never hear the music of the cosmos.' I looked at the girl, wondering if I was laying it on too thick. She was listening intent, no sign of cynicism. I went on. 'I've been south. I've seen the home counties around London. Nothing but roads and traffic and urban sprawl, with a few fields fighting to find fresh air amongst it all.' It was twisting the knife, but I didn't care. 'We can't have that happen here.'

Her sharp eyes belied her dolly girl looks. 'Yes, I understand. But that's the growth of population. How do you stop that?'

'Ah well, that's a whole other thing. Don't ask me about that.'

'Mars,' said Danny, breaking the mood.

Collins blinked at him, then went on. 'Yes, but that's the problem. More people, more wealth, and all wanting more houses. That's why companies like ours need more stone.'

'Ay, well... you'll have to find it elsewhere,' I grunted. 'By the way – did you see the photos of our flood?'

'Yes.' He didn't elaborate.

'Doesn't that affect your plans?'

He hesitated. 'Well, it might be a problem.'

'Unless of course having the rail up on an embankment means it isn't.'

He had the grace to look embarrassed. 'Who told you that?'

'The council surveyors. They came after the floods. So is it part of the plan?'

I was pleased to watch his discomfort. 'Well... across some parts, yes. We might need one – to keep it level.'

'You never revealed that before. That increases our problem, wouldn't you say?'

His discomfort increased.

'Canal,' said Danny.

He blinked, and threw Danny a vaguely startled look. The turned back. 'I told my father we should explain, but he said not to mention it until we were certain.'

Pretty feeble excuse. I stayed deadpan, but to change the subject I said, 'Why were you at the council offices?'

'Oh... just finalising some planning details.' He scratched his nail on one of the wall top stones, where people had carved their initials.

He had none of his father's forthright bluntness. 'We got your lawyer's list of possible objections. Quite an opus. He seems to know his stuff.'

'Yes,' I replied. I didn't say I'd never met the man.

Danny had got bored with the conversation, and was wandering along the walls looking for fossils, carvings, insects.

Collins looked up with a more frank expression now. 'If it was up to me, I'd pull out. It's not worth the hassle.'

Annie's eyebrows went up. 'Really?'

He threw her a glance. 'But my father's different. He doesn't give up. I think he enjoys a fight.'

'So what does he intend?' she said.

He shrugged. The shrug of a man familiar with irresistible forces and immovable objects. 'We're quite powerful. He's got a lot of friends in high places. He can get things pushed through despite the objections.'

I said, 'And if it stirs up local opposition? If people come out in force?'

'As I said, he likes a fight. He doesn't mind using the law and the police to force things through, even if there's trench war on the streets.'

I had the impression his relationship with his father wasn't always as smooth as double cream. I turned away and strolled alone down the walkway on the walls. They followed. Nothing was said until we came across a plaque detailing the history of the castle. Collins stopped to read it, and Annie joined him, pointing out stuff. I and the girl wandered on.

'Have you been engaged long?' I asked, for want of polite conversation.

'Oh, we've been together for a year or two,' she said. 'Fiancée was just being polite.'

'Ah.'

'We met through business. I'm in finance, they need finance. We need people who need finance.'

'We all need finance.'

'Yes.' Her skirt rippled in the breeze. 'I shouldn't say this...' She glanced back at him. 'But you need to be careful.'

'Why?'

'His father can be tough. I've seen it.'

'Tough?'

'Ruthless.'

I looked at her sideways. 'Have you been sent along to soften us up?'

Her grey eyes twinkled sharply at me. 'No. Nothing like that. I'm just warning you. Martin isn't like that. In fact he's a bit of a softy.' She gazed at the distant landscape. 'Too soft sometimes.'

I wondered what that meant, but didn't ask. 'Unlike his father.'

'He's a different animal.'

I sniffed the air. It was subtly different here in the rural town, to the farm. 'Well, I'm not equipped to tackle tycoons. But we can be tough in Yorkshire too.'

She copied my sniff. I bet the air was different to what she was used to too. I noticed she wore minimal makeup. 'I'm sure you can,' she said. 'But you need to be clever too.'

She had me puzzled. 'Aren't you on their side?'

'I'm on no one's side. But I understand what you were saying. I do love your landscape.'

I warmed to her further. Whether it was the comment or the grey eyes, I wasn't sure. But I wasn't going to be fooled. I knew all about honey traps.

I glanced back. Her boyfriend and Annie were still chatting closely over the plaque. Danny was ahead of us, engrossed in his investigations. We walked on.

'What happened to your arm?' she asked, casually as if asking about a bee sting. People rarely asked that.

'Just farming,' I said. 'Accident with machinery.' It wasn't the whole truth, but it was what I told people.

She looked sympathetic. 'How awful.'

'It's all right. I never think of it now.'

Cumulus clouds were gathering off to the west, like nuclear

mushrooms. 'Rain later,' I said.

'You depend a lot on the weather, don't you?'

'Yes. It's everything. Weather and people.'

She chuckled. 'Ah well, we all depend on people.'

The others caught us up. 'Interesting history,' said Martin. 'I wonder how many other castles there are still standing in Britain.'

'Hundreds,' I said. 'Literally. Most half ruined like this. People took the stones to build their big houses with. Shame that. Some of the houses are a lot uglier than the castles.'

Julia said, 'Well, at least it meant they can't have been fighting each other any more.'

'I suppose so. But he who is ignorant of history is doomed to repeat it, as somebody said.'

Annie threw me her condescending look. It said, 'Stop being pretentious.'

We headed for the exit gate across the wide lawns of the castle bailey. House martins were swooping around the ruins. Only a couple of other tourists were in sight, studying their guide book. We reached the car park, and I whistled to Danny. He abandoned his studies and joined us. They were in a high-powered sports job. Danny of course knew the make, model, and engine size, which impressed them further.

As they were climbing in, Collins pointed a finger over the roof. 'Just have a think about it,' he said. 'No point going to war over it. No point building castles.'

'Tell your father, no point bringing battering rams.'

He gave a wry smile, directed at us both. We waved them goodbye as they drove off.

'They seemed nice,' said Annie.

'Yes.'

'So what do you think he wanted?'

'I'm not sure. I don't know if he knew himself.' I glanced sideways at her. 'Did he say anything to you?'

She shook her head. 'We just talked history. He's an interesting man under the smooth suits.'

'Interesting?'

'More worldly than he seems. He's into other stuff than making money.'

'Such as?'

She shrugged. 'Oh, just generally. He understands your position better than you think.'

For some reason I didn't like the way the conversation was going. 'Good for him,' was all I could say.

She lowered her lids at me. 'Did she say anything to you?'

'Not much. Just that the father could be tough.'

'Well, we knew that.'

'And she understood my position too.'

'Good for her.'

'She was pretty,' said Danny.

CHAPTER THIRTEEN

fryday. 7.04. nise day. 19C. yestiday wos the best day ever we went to barnard casil mum and dad and me. mum and me went to the museem wich is my no 3 favrit place after the zoo and the train. then we went on the casil wich is anuther favrit place. it was bilt in 1095 and I fownd a red admral caterpiler on the wall but i didnt bring it bac for my colecshin. i tried to do that one time but i cudnt make it hatch into a red admral buter fly wich is my favrit. it needs to be free. we met sum nice peepil there from lundun a very prity lady and they had a audi r8 sports car with a 5 leeter engin. mumdad had an argiment abowt them but i didn no why

I came out into the yard early next morning, and something was wrong.

I didn't know what, but I just sensed that things weren't normal. I stood in the yard, smelt the air, looked around, but could detect nothing. Just the usual smells and breezes and distant horizons.

Then it hit me. There were no sounds from the far fellside. There was usually something coming from there. Distant sheep calls, bird cries, rock cracks, the melody of nature. Today, nothing.

I fetched my binoculars from the buggy, and scanned the hillside. Not a sheep to be seen.

Old Jim came up from his cottage as I was looking. 'What's up?' he said.

'I don't know. Can't see any sheep. Let's go and look.'

We got into the buggy with Trigger, and I drove fast to the hillside. Climbed to the top wall and drove around the wide fell. Clouds and wind and waving grasses, but no sheep. Even the birds seemed to have deserted.

There were only three ways out through the dry-stone walls. One at the far western edge, which was permanently closed; the gate onto the main track leading to the lane, padlocked after my encounter with the trespassers; and the gate to the farm-yard track, which was the one we'd come through, and which was secure. We approached the one to the lane. It was swinging wide open. Hadn't needed a battering ram either.

I stopped beside it, and we examined the padlock. The chain had been cut. The newly trampled earth all around the opening told its own story.

'Bastards!' I said, gazing impotently up the track towards the lane two hundred yards away. 'Who the fuck...?'

Jim was studying the ground beyond the gate. 'Look here, boss,' he said. He had called me boss for fifteen years and wasn't going to stop now.

I joined him, and he pointed at the new tyre marks in the mud at the side of the track. 'Looks like a truck or a Land Rover.' He leaned down closer. 'And see there. His nearside front tyre's still got plenty o' tread, but his offside's worn almost bare. Never get past the MOT, that wouldn't.'

'Huh!' I exclaimed. 'It's the Faulkners, ten to one. They're the only ones round here who don't maintain anything.' I looked back at the lane. 'They must have come in the night. Do you suppose the sheep are all...?'

'We'd better go and look,' he said, climbing back into the buggy.

As I got in myself, my smart phone rang.

'Hello.'

'Roger?' It was my other neighbouring farmer, a mile up the lane. Mike Foster, a decent sort and a good farmer. 'We've got a mass of sheep wandering about all over the road and the heath round here. Your markings. Have you left a gate open?'

'We've had a bit of sabotage,' I said. 'I'm on my way.'

We drove down the lane. No other traffic at that time of morning. Sure enough, we soon came upon stray sheep grazing on the verges. One or two at first, then more and more. As we approached Foster's farm there was a wide space of open heath, and here around two hundred animals were scattered, having the feast of their lives. God knows how many poisonous plants they were sampling.

It took us most of the morning, with Mike Foster's tractor and Trigger's sprinting, to get them all together, and herded back down the lane to their rightful home. When we counted them through the gate, there were at least three missing, maybe more.

Mike, sitting on his tractor, ruddy face sweating, said, 'Do you know how they got out?'

'I've a fair idea,' I said.

'Is this summat to do with your railway business?'

'It might be.'

'Well, if it was humans did it, you need to string them from the nearest tree.' He started his tractor again, then turned in the seat and shouted over the motor, 'There's an NFU meeting next week. D'you want to bring it up with the committee?'

He was vice-chairman of the local branch of the farmer's union. I said, 'I won't be there this time, Mike. Too much to do. Can you do it?'

He nodded. 'Why not? Although maybe they'd all like rail lines if the money's good.'

He grinned, turned his tractor, and headed off home. He had a smaller farm than ours, but good land mostly, and he knew what it was all about. He was rooted in the soil as we all were.

Jim and I stood by the gate, watching the flock disperse again over the hillside. 'Keep an eye on them, Jim.' I said. 'There was milkweed, birdsfoot, god knows what around that heath. Any signs of vomiting or lethargy, and we'll get the vet here sharp.'

He nodded. I looked at the tyre marks again, now almost trampled away. 'Those bloody Faulkners. I'm going to see them.' I turned back to the buggy.

'Careful, boss,' said Jim. 'Don't go on your own.'

'They don't scare me.' I drove down to the yard to get the jeep.

I don't rise to temper easily. I'm a slow burner. By the time I reached the Faulkner farm the slow burn had heated to a furnace. As

I drove into their yard, one of the two sons was doing something with their own battered utility, the other was aimlessly kicking a football against the brick wall of a shed. Old man Faulkner was nowhere to be seen. They both looked up as I skidded to a halt beside their vehicle.

I got out, and walked slowly to the front of their rusting heap without saying a word. I stooped and looked at the front tyres. Sure enough, one was newish, thick treaded, the other worn almost bare.

I straightened up. They were both watching me with expressionless faces. Big lads, almost as tall as me, but already with beer bellies and pasty complexions.

'You owe me three sheep,' I said.

'Who says?' The one closest to me drooped his eyelids. He wasn't scared.

'I say. You let all my sheep out of pasture, and by the time we got them back, at least three were missing. And if any have eaten poisoned plants, you might owe me more.'

He leaned casually against the cab of the truck. His brother had approached closer.

'How d'you know it was us?'

'It was you.'

'Where's your proof?'

I pointed at his tyres. 'There's the proof. Tyre marks all over the gateway. Pretty stupid mistake that.' The flicker of a frown crossed his face. 'And I bet you've left the wire cutters still in the back there.'

He threw a look at the other one, who was now standing about five yards away. Then looked back. The frown had changed to a smirk. 'So what you gonna do about it?'

The thing is, people think I'm a pushover because I'm crippled. They don't realise that makes me tougher than I ever was when I had both arms. And they don't know my history. What's more, bar room brawlers are used to warding off right-handed punches mostly. They get taken by surprise by one coming from the left.

I punched him knuckle-hard in the chest, right over his heart. That's a real pressure point. He went down like a stick in a gale. His brother came at me, wide-eyed. Before he could swing I punched him too, in the mouth. Teeth splintered along with my knuckles, and he went down too, spitting blood and yelping like a wounded puppy.

'Hoy!' The back door to the farmhouse had opened, and Brad Faulkner came out, staring. I walked towards him, giving one of the sons a sharp kick in the ribs for good measure as I passed. Brad pulled up short, gazing at me like a startled heifer.

'What the...?'

'So, Brad,' I said, nursing my bloody knuckles. 'Resorted to sabotage now, have you?'

'No, I... what d'you mean?'

'You know bloody well what I mean.' I was up to him now, face to face. 'I don't know whether it was just your boys, or whether you were with them, but either way two can play at that game. I'll be sending you a bill for my missing sheep, and if I find any of you anywhere near my land again, I'll be back, and I'll burn your whole bloody farm to the ground. Preferably with you in it.'

He found some courage then, and stuck his ship's prow chin out. 'I warned you, Oldfield. We all need this deal. Don't you threaten me. I've got far bigger forces behind me than you can muster, and if you don't give way then a few missing sheep won't be all you'll have to worry about.'

I stared into his ailing goat's eyes for several seconds. 'So... this was prompted by the Collins's then?'

He hesitated. 'I didn't say that. I'm just telling you that a lot of people and a lot of interests want to see this railway, and you're not going to be able to stand up against them all.'

'How d'you think letting my flock loose is going to change things?'

'That's just a warning. That's just letting you know what might happen if you carry on. You're just a small-time farmer with a stupid obsession about a worthless piece of countryside, and there's no way you can fight today's world.'

I glanced round at his sons. They were still on the ground, recovering. I was glad to see one of them had fallen into a patch of cow dung. 'Worthless piece of countryside, is it?' I said. 'Well, you may consider your piece of countryside worthless, Brad. And the way you farm it, it probably is. But let me tell you, mine is worth a lot more than money, or stone quarries, or railways, or bloody gold mines. Mine is priceless. So don't you come anywhere near it again, or I'll be digging your grave on it.'

I turned away, walked back past the semi-prostrate sons to my jeep, and drove off. They couldn't see, but I was suddenly shaking. The encounter had brought back memories from another era, another land, which I had thought I had erased from memory.

CHAPTER FOURTEEN

satiday. 18.24. 24C. dad very cros today sumwun let all the sheep owt of the top feelds. didn do mi leson this morning bicos he had to find them. he sed ther ar not nise peepl in the wurld. i no that becos they are not nise to me sum times. also not nise diner tinite. evry body quiit. i lisen to my mozart piano 21

Some days after my visit to the Faulkner farm, I learned of another visit there.

Big Fred the vet was passing by our way, and dropped in for a tot and a chat as he was wont to do. After the obligatory queries after the animals, the obligatory glass, and the obligatory flirtation with Annie, he said, 'I had to go to the Faulkners yesterday. Usual problems with their flock because they don't follow my instructions.' His big lip curled. 'Useless bunch. Anyway, when I drove in there was a car just leaving. Big silver-grey limmo, would you believe. Never seen the like at their place before. When I asked old man Faulkner who it was, he just waved it away. Said it was people interested in doing business with him.' Fred snorted. 'Likely story. But then of course I realised. It was probably some of your lot and their railway. They need to cross his land too, don't they?'

'Yes,' I said. 'Just the corner of it, but they've offered money, and of course he's keen to accept. We've had words about it.' I didn't add we'd had fists about it too.

'Ay, well they're obviously in thick with him. Didn't seem like Londoners though. Lancashire plates on the car.'

I frowned. 'Could you see who was in it?'

'No. Tinted windows. But there were two or three.'

My father was sitting with us in the kitchen, having heard Fred arrive. 'Buggers!' he said. 'Bloody foreigners muscling in everywhere.' To my father, everyone outside North Yorks was a foreigner.

'Offering big money though,' said Fred. He eyed Dad shrewdly. They'd known each other for half a century. 'What do you feel about it, Bill?'

Dad sniffed, and stared into his coffee mug. 'Not up to me. It's up to Roger there. He's the boss now. But if it was me...' He tailed off.

'What?' demanded Fred.

'I dunno. It's tempting. Times are changing.'

'Dad!' I exclaimed.

He shrugged, and rubbed at his arthritic wrist. 'Well, can you fight off today's world for ever?'

I was tired of hearing that. 'Isn't that the point?' I said. I waved at the outside. 'Let today's world in, and we'll lose the old world for ever. You of all people know that.'

'Ay, well... I'm glad it's not me deciding.'

'Me neither,' said the vet. Downed the last of his whiskey. 'Well, I guess our generation has had its day, Bill. But mebbe we should do our bit to help the next one.' He heaved his great bulk out of the chair. 'Anyway, I just thought I should tell you. They're marshallin' their forces. God knows what they're planning, but you need to be prepared.'

I phoned up the London lawyer recommended by Sir Peter. More for a bit of moral support than anything else. I said, 'Are you getting anywhere with our situation, Mr Driscoll? We're getting a lot of pressure at this end.'

He didn't sound quite so buoyant this time. 'Well, I fired a strong opening salvo. Got a polite acknowledgement, but nothing else. Followed it up with a reminder, but got no reply. So I made a few enquiries. Seems they are lobbying the Minister for Transport, the Minister for the Environment, and the Minister for Industry. Probably the Minister for Funny Hats too. They seem to have some influence around Whitehall because of their various projects on behalf of government. They appear determined to try and push this through.

'So we might have to lodge formal objections?'

'It's beginning to look that way.' His tone sounded sympathetic. I couldn't picture what he looked like on the other end. 'It's not a difficult process, but gathering evidence, getting witnesses and so on, can take a bit of time.'

'And expense.'

'Well, you can do most of the work once I've advised you what to go for. Try and get up a petition also, with all the local signatures you can muster.' His voice lowered. 'Of course the enemy won't want an official inquiry any more than you do. It could delay things for quite a while.'

'That's why they're playing dirty tricks to persuade me.'

'Is that's what's happening?'

'Seems so.' I didn't go into details.

'Well, keep a record. Witnesses, evidence, photos. It could be useful.'

'Right.'

'And there's something else you can do. Do you know your local MP?'

'I've met him.'

'Well, get on to him. He should be on your side. He could be your ally in Westminster.'

Our MP was a Tory man. Rural Yorkshire is traditionally Tory. The cities and coal mine areas are Labour, especially after Margaret Thatcher closed the mines and had the police playing at gladiators with the miners on the streets. Country people are more self-sufficient and independent. They don't like big government meddling in their affairs.

However the Stainbridge quarry was over the border in the next constituency. I reckoned that was where I needed to start. I'd met their man a few times, mostly on farming issues. He was a dour cove. Tall and thin, face like a camel with indigestion, but he wasn't stupid. I imagined he'd be on my side. I got an appointment at his next surgery. It was his last before the summer recess.

When I walked into his office, wearing a jacket and tie for the second time in months, he was looking at some documents with an overweight but sexy looking secretary. They both laughed at something he was saying, then he saw me and said, 'Thanks, Carol, sort it for me,' and he smacked her large bottom as she went off giggling. I thought MPs didn't dare do that sort of thing these days, but then this is Yorkshire, and anything goes here.

He put his stern face on again as he shook my hand over the desk, and said, 'Hello, Roger. Haven't seen you for a while. What are you doing in our constituency?'

I sat opposite him. 'You presumably know about the Stainbridge quarry plan?'

'Yes, of course.'

'What's your opinion?'

He looked a bit taken aback at the blunt question. Probably used to convoluted parliamentary queries requiring convoluted answers. He said, 'Well, it's a big project of course. It'll bring quite a bit of work to the area.'

'Not to say some income presumably.'

'Probably, yes.'

'But the railway. What about the railway?'

'What about it?' When asked a difficult question, always answer with another one.

'You know it would go right through my farm.'

He gazed out of the window for a second, although there wasn't much to see out there. He knew of course. 'Would you like a coffee?'

'No, thanks. What I'd like is your opinion.'

He looked back at me, beady-eyed. 'I imagine they've offered you compensation.'

'Yes. That's not the issue.'

'What is the issue?'

'The issue is rail lines ploughing through the Dales. Some of it through your constituency.'

He sat still again, nodding his camel head. 'Yes. I understand your feelings.'

'Haven't you had reactions from your own constituents?'

'Well, you see, it's not quite such a controversial matter here. The route is mainly outside the area of natural beauty. Until it gets to you, that is.'

'Oh, so railways can only go through ugly places.'

'That's not what I'm saying.'

'It's setting a hell of a precedent.'

'Mm.'

I was getting the feeling that this wouldn't be as simple as I'd imagined. 'Can't you see the furore this would cause?'

More nodding. 'Yes, it's a tricky one, Roger. I can see your point of view. On the other hand, it's a big commercial enterprise. It's the modern world.'

'I keep hearing that. The modern world. Does that mean it's a good thing?'

'I don't know. It's progress versus aesthetics.'

I began to bridle now. 'This is much more than aesthetics.' I could hear the sound of laughter coming from the outer office. Happy staff apparently. 'What's the thinking around Westminster? It's presumably doing the various ministry rounds?'

'Yes, yes. It's being considered by all the relevant departments.'

'Come on, Geoffrey. You must know the general opinion.'

He sighed and looked around. A camel looking for water. 'Well, I'll be honest, Roger. The corridors of power are more interested in progressing the economy than in saving a strip of distant moorland. And the company involved are pulling lots of levers. The fact of the matter is that everyone is waiting to see what objections will be raised locally. They all know that is where the battle will be fought, if there is to be a battle.'

'You bet there'll be a battle. That's why I'm here. I want to know what side of the battle you're on.'

'You're really putting me on the spot, aren't you?'

'Yes.'

'Have you spoken to your own MP?'

'He's a minister. The quarry's your baby. I wanted to speak to you first.'

He squeezed his long nose, as if trying to make it longer. 'Very well. The answer is I don't know which side I'm on yet. The project would be good for my constituency, but controversial in yours and elsewhere. I'm between a rock and a hard place. I'm biding my time to see how things pan out.'

'I thought politicians were supposed to be decisive.'

He allowed himself a lopsided smile. 'Ah, how innocent you are. The art of politics is to never be decisive until the decision looks inevitable, and then to make it appear that you're the one who made it.'

Another burst of giggles next door. I got up. 'Well, I don't seem to be any the wiser.'

He rose too. His eyes showed a trace of sympathy. 'In the end it will all come down to public opinion, Roger. Farmers and land lovers, versus business and employment figures. You'll need to run a good campaign.'

'I'll run a clean campaign. The questions is, will they?'

He hesitated. 'Are they playing dirty?'

'Possibly.'

'Ah.' He glowered down the nose. 'Well, keep me informed.'

'I will.'

I left with that small crumb of encouragement. The modern world. I know I'm a Luddite, but, like a twisted worm trying to find its own tail, it's too distorted for its own good.

CHAPTER FIFTEEN

fryday. 11.47. cold. 16C. playd monoply with grampa. i got 2 hotels on the green and 6 houses on the orinj but he wun. lily playd cards wen she got bac from scool and i wun at blacjac but she wun at wist. peeple always wont to win. at cards or rail ways. i askd lily why. she sed its so they can get better at stuf. seems a funy way to me. shepids pie agen for diner. triger was alowd sum its his no 1 favrit

'I want a holiday.'

Annie was struggling in from the back with an armful of logs she could hardly see over. We liked to stack up the Inglenook hearth in summer when they were dry. We'd go through them like a forest fire once the evenings chilled. It was one of the jobs I couldn't do.

'You need a holiday too,' she gasped as she dropped them with a clatter in the stone hearth. 'We all need to get in a holiday from this bloody farm and this bloody business. Before it starts getting too cold to swim.'

That's one of the disadvantages of farming. You can never get away from it. The cows won't stop milking, or the sheep straying, just because you need a break. We had from time to time managed to play truant for a week or two, by hiring in a professional manager to aid Jim, but I was always apprehensive as to what calamity might unfold in my absence.

But she was right. We all needed a break. The kids too. It was the end of the school holiday period, and they rarely got to go elsewhere like other kids do. They didn't complain too much, but they always looked wistful when the holiday ads came on the telly – all golden sands and swimming pools and naked people. For me, all that seemed a waste of life's moments, but I knew that was being selfish.

'Where?' I asked. I was sitting in my armchair by the bow window, looking out over the fells with a mug of sweet tea beside me. I was mentally exhausted after a fortnight of gathering evidence for the appeal. Reports, statistics, testimonials, surveys – enough paperwork to keep all Westminster busy. Most of it meaningless.

'Anywhere,' she said, brushing wood chips off her apron. 'Anywhere where it's warm, and we can see the sea, and you don't have to work and I don't have to cook.'

'I don't want to go abroad,' I said. 'Not with this going on.'

'Who suggested abroad? We've got all the British Isles to choose from.'

Yes, well there were other places besides Yorkshire. 'Shall I see if Tom Preece has one of his cottages free?'

She smiled then. The smile she knew churned me over every time. Tom Preece was a fellow farmer in Cornwall, who let out holiday cottages as a side-line. We'd been there a few times. It was a long drive – well over three hundred miles south – but when you got there, the air was like warm chablis, the beaches were wide and skin-scorching sandy, his cottages were on the clifftops with widescreen views across the incoming surf.

She said, 'We'll be lucky. The whole of London heads for Cornwall in the summer hols.'

'No, they all go to the Costa del Sol or Monte Carlo these days. I'll call him.'

Tom liked having us there. He and I could spend hours talking farm stuff whilst the others were down on the beach or roaming the cliffs. He hesitated when I rang.

'You've left it a bit late, Roger.'

'I know. Last minute decision, sorry.'

'We're pretty booked up, but if you can make it next weekend, we've had a cancellation on the Oregano Cottage. It's the small one, so you'd have to all cram in.'

'We'll cram into your hen house if it means we can come,' I said.

'No that's already booked up. But I look forward to seeing you. Next Sunday if that's good.'

'That's good.'

I shut off the phone and looked at Annie. The smile got bigger.

Lily would be happy because they kept a couple of horses, and Danny was always happy when he had different animals to mingle with, and rock pools to do his forensic studies on. We asked Dad if he wanted to come, but he said he was past tramping moors and freezing his arse off in English seas.

I had another reason to visit Tom. Two years previously he'd had his own run-in with the authorities over a right of way. The local council, under pressure from the various hikers bodies, wanted to divert the ancient coastal path which ran behind his farm, to cross his land along the cliff top. He objected because it would mean serious intrusion onto his pastures, and all sorts of hassle from illicit campers and the more disorderly species of wanderer. There were already miles of clifftop routes in that area, so he wasn't depriving anyone of sea views. He had fought them off. I wanted to know how he did it.

I found someone to stand in for me at the farm, gave instructions to Jim, and the four of us packed into my creaking Ford Galaxy. It was well weathered, but it had a big old engine and made no complaints about the journey. We set off early morning that Sunday, the car stuffed with enough gear to furnish an Everest expedition, and headed south. Explorers abandoning the homestead.

It took us all day, Annie and me sharing the driving. Eight hours including stops, but the further we went, the brighter got the skies, the warmer got the air. Surprising how much higher the temperature gets with every southerly stretch of road. And how much higher get the passengers. They'd sung every Abba song in the book by the time we reached Cornwall. Danny's piercing discords hurt the ears, but it kept him happy. The last twenty miles were mostly single-track lanes winding between high banks of fern, wild flowers, and blackberry thickets with the berries not yet ripe. Spoiled only by glimpses of massed giant wind turbines scarring the skies inland.

We were all pretty worn by the time we got there, but as soon as we climbed out of the car in front of the low whitewashed farmhouse, the late-afternoon sunshine hit us like a bonfire exploding, the sea air had us high again within minutes, the seagull cries filled our ears like a Sibelius concert with a bad conductor.

'Yes!' said Annie.

'Yes!' said Lily.

Danny was studying the sea horizon through his binoculars already. Looking for whales probably.

Tom and his wife, Betty, came out of the house as I was searching in the back for the gift gin I'd brought. He, gnarled, creased, and creaking at the knees – she, stout, pink, and still with her naughty fifth-form face. We all embraced like relatives coming together.

'You've not changed,' said Tom to me.

'Nor have you,' I lied.

'You've got younger,' said Betty to Annie.

'You've lost weight,' said Annie.

'And as for you...' said Tom, looking at Lily. 'Christ! Has Hollywood come knockin' yet?'

Lily smiled demurely.

'Have you still got the goats?' demanded Danny.

'We sure have,' said Betty. 'And I'm badly needing someone to help with the milking.'

He grinned his toothy grin.

Tom held out keys. 'The cottage is ready. You know your way about. Evening drinks at six.' That's what I liked about him. Straight to the point, no frills.

The other three walked the couple of hundred yards down the track towards the sea, whilst I drove the car there. The tiny cottage was one of three, ranged across the cliff top. Built two centuries ago for farm hands, or maybe fishermen, but now worth their weight in platinum. Solid as boulders, but inside opened up and all mod cons, each with their own front terrace and potted plants, and their own patch of windswept garden. Tom could have retired on the income from them alone. But he was a farmer, and farmers don't retire until they can't get out of bed.

Annie and I had the one decent sized bedroom with Impressionists on the wall and the obligatory four-poster, Lily had the other one, where there was a chest of drawers and just room to get around the bed, and Danny had the couch-bed in the living area, which suited him fine because he could wander outside in the night without disturbing anyone. He had strict instructions not to go beyond the white fence that ran along the cliff-top.

Lily and I brought in all the gear whilst Annie boiled the kettle for tea. We didn't unpack, just sat out on the terrace with our mugs, inhaling everything like opium. The sky and the sea were wider than galaxies.

'Beats Yorkshire,' said Annie.

'Don't you dare,' I said.

'Well... let's say the weather does.'

'Hah! You haven't been in a Cornish sea gale.'

We watched the gulls swirling, the heather rippling, the waves parading. Even Danny was quiet.

That night I slept better than I had done for weeks. Partly because the drive had tired me, partly because the sea air drugged me, and partly because Annie had raped me with even more enthusiasm than usual. We just hoped Lily couldn't hear us and the four-poster creaking through the stone walls.

The next day, they all wanted to head straight for the beach. I sent them off with enough sandwiches to feed the Household Cavalry, and said I'd join them a bit later. Then Tom and I sat on his porch with our coffee, the Celtic skies drowning us in blue, and discussed the state of the world.

After exchanging our productivity statistics, slandering the current Minister for Agriculture, and fantasising about retiring to the Caribbean, I told him my railway story.

'Hm,' he murmured, his weathered gnome's face creased into the shape of a Cornish pasty. 'That's a bugger.'

'You had a situation a year or two back over the coastal trail. How did you beat them on that?'

He squinted sideways at me with a sly expression. Then he took a long swig at his coffee. Never one to leap in was Tom.

'Well, it's true, I was up against it over that.' His accent was drawled West Country, thick as peat. 'They'd got the council on board, the Country Landowners, Friends of The Earth, friends of blurry everybody. I thought we were going to lose all this.' He waved at the untainted view across the turf all the way to the Milky Way. 'So I put the grey cells to work and came up with a plan. Pure Machiavelli it was.'

'What was that?'

He scratched his hedgehog stubble. 'This is confidential, moind. First of all we put up every objection and every appeal we could think of, to hold things up. Then I had a mate who was on my side, and we got him to join the local walkers club. They were the ones leadin' the campaign. He deliberately stirred things up, and provoked them to a demonstration at my boundary over there, with a planned march right across the cliff edge. They can be pretty aggressive, these hikers. Bad as the hunt saboteurs, and the animal rights lot. Then 'e let me know when it was going to happen.'

He stopped, and threw me another sly fox grin.

'And?' I said.

'We'd already reinforced the fences there – put barbed wire along the top, and barricaded the gate. We also saw to it there were a few sheep in that first field. Then I got in a reporter on the local paper with the bait that he'd have a good story. He and his photographer, and me with my video camera, hid behind the cow shed and waited. Sure enough the mob arrived – about fifty of them. They milled around outside the fence, shoutin' and wavin' silly banners, and that. Then my friend urged them on, and they broke through the gate like a herd of bullocks, and came runnin' right across to the far side. The sheep of course belted off bleating like a brass band, and we captured the whole thing on camera. Made a real song and dance about it. He got a full page spread, I got my video on the local TV news, and they interviewed me weepin' crocodile tears about how the hooligans had wrecked my fences, stampeded my animals, and caused untold damage to the entire British farming industry.' He snorted. 'The plan was dropped without a murmur.'

'You old devil,' I said.

'Don't tell anyone mind. 'Specially not Betty. She don't approve of that kind of thing.'

'Didn't she know?'

'Not that I'd contrived the whole business.'

We were silent, savouring the moment. Butterflies hovered. The sea mumbled in the background.

Then I said, 'Am I wrong, Tom?'

'Wrong?'

'To fight against what's happening. Am I just being contrarian – stuck in another era?'

He watched a kestrel hovering above the small world. 'Depends. Depends whether it were a better era than this one.' Tom was an avid reader. He had enough books in the house to fill the British Library. 'Sometimes you wonder.'

'Yes, that's the whole question, isn't it? I look at people today, obsessed with their social media, and their tabloid stories, and their crass TV shows, and I wonder whether we're not just going back to a digital stone age.'

He grunted. 'Most people have alus been donkeys. Nowadays they're just fat donkeys.' He took a swig at his coffee and nibbled on a home-made muffin. 'I asked a local councillor the other day, what he thought about the theory of evolution. He looked at me as if I was speaking Japanese. Mind you, his wife said she was all for it, and had been waiting twenty years for him to evolve. So perhaps there are some bright people.'

I had to chuckle. 'Well, anyway, I don't think I could invent anything over my problem as crafty as you did, but I can probably get a lot of opposition up amongst the local farming community.'

'Well, it's how you do it that counts. You have to get the occasion right, and the timin' right. Pretty girls lying in front of bulldozers sort of thing. You need to be sure the media know about it, and get as much publicity as possible. No point creating a hullabaloo in a vacuum.'

'No.'

Then he glinted at me. "Course you could take them on single-handedly.'

'I've heard that joke a hundred times, Tom.'

'Yeh. Sorry.'

The days drifted by in a dream of surf and sand and sybaritic pleasures. We plagued the beaches, wandered the lanes, marauded the countryside. We rode Tom's horses over the fields, played beach cricket, invaded the village pubs. Annie got sun burned and fat, Lily galloped Tom's big hunter after imaginary foxes, Danny vanished into the animal sheds for hours at a time. And I began to relax. Maybe holidays weren't so bad after all.

But on the fifth morning I got a call on my mobile.

'Boss, we've got a problem.' It was old Jim. It took something serious to get him on the phone.

'What's happened?'

'It's the cows. They're all sick. Someone's poisoned the water.'

My mind did a somersault. 'Poisoned?'

'I reckon so. It's the water. In the troughs. I reckon someone's spiked the beck high up.'

Our troughs were fed directly from the small water sources that filtered down from the high fells. Clear as crystal usually, and didn't often dry up.

'Do you know who? Where?'

'No. Can't prove anything. Could have been anywhere up the slopes.'

'Those bloody Faulkners again.'

'Mebbe. But might have been anyone.'

'Is the vet there?'

'Yeh. He's treating them. But two heifers are in a bad way. He's sent the water to be analysed.'

I untangled my brain. 'I'll come straight back, Jim. I'll leave the family here and catch the train.'

'Sorry to spoil yer holiday, boss.'

'Don't worry. I'll see you tonight.'

CHAPTER SIXTEEN

sun day 21.11 nite. 14C. we are on holyday in corn wol. its my and lilys no 1 playc. im alowd to go in the beech pools ther and find crabs and lots of shels and stuf for my colecshin. they hav gotes and gees wich we dont hav and bety lets me help milk the gotes. the ownly bad thing was dad had to go home erly becos the cows wer sic. i sed fred the vet cud look after them but dad sed he had to go and i had a tan trum. the farm al ways spoils things

The two heifers had to be put down, and the milking herd took a week to recover. It took me longer. An assault like that on one's animals is like an assault on one's family. It spears to the guts and leaves one reeling as if poisoned also.

The tests confirmed that it was something with an unpronounceable chemical name introduced into the tanks. We started testing the water last thing at night and first thing in the morning, but of course they weren't going to pull the same trick twice. I went up the water courses on the hillside looking for clues, but it was an impossible quest. No tell-tale tyre marks this time, and no gates had been broken open.

I pondered as to who had done it. The Faulkners were the obvious suspects, but somehow I had doubts. They would be too vulnerable to police investigation, especially after their last stunt. The Dragonsmead people would surely not try something like that directly. Had they commissioned a third party? If so this thing had taken a new turn.

I talked again to the London lawyer, and told him what had happened.

'Ah, they're playing dirty,' he said.

'What could they hope to gain from a trick like that?' I asked.

'It's all a steady campaign to wear you down. Put stress on yourselves and on your finances, and force you to accept their offer. They don't want it to go to judicial review any more than you do.'

I contemplated the implications. 'So we can expect more?'

'Possibly. How is your appeal package going?'

'More or less ready. I've got all the environment reports, and an online petition with around a thousand signatures from local people. Also a number of personal comments from other farmers. Quite fun reading.'

'Fun?'

I read him a few. 'You put a rail through our land, and we'll drive herds of cows up Whitehall.' 'The gravestones of politicians are all made of limestone.' 'Spoil our lovely Dales, and we'll paint Big Ben purple.' That sort of thing.'

He was chuckling. 'And they thought the civil wars were a thing of the past. Did you get one from Sir Peter?'

'Yes, he's written a brilliant protest.'

'Seen your MP yet?'

'No. Saw the next constituency's, where the quarry lies. He's sitting on the fence. Ours is in the Cabinet, and I'm not sure how to approach him.'

'Well, leave that to me. Meanwhile get everything into a professional looking file.'

'Are we going to lodge it?'

'Not yet. Once that's done, it becomes official and there's no going back. First of all we send it to Dragonsmead. Show them what they're up against.'

'Won't that be giving our game away?'

'Well, they'll get it all anyway once formalities start. Best to put pressure on before it gets that far. That's what they're doing to you.' There was a rustle of paper on the other end. 'Hm, I see the deadline for your appeal is approaching. We need to delay. Have you reported the poisoning business to the police?'

'No. There didn't seem much point.'

'Well, I suggest you do so. Give them any evidence you have –

chemical analysis and so on. Then we can use their investigation into dirty deeds as an excuse to postpone the appeal.'

Devious. The ways of the law are manifold. I was glad I had him on our side. Especially when the next event occurred.

It was some days later. The family had returned from Cornwall, sunburnt, sea-stained, wind-seared. It was late at night. Everyone had gone to bed, and I was in the bathroom, preparing to do so myself, and wondering whether it was too late to interrupt Annie's nodding off, when there was a shriek from Lily's bedroom.

'Dad! The hay barn's on fire!'

Her window looked in that direction, and the flare had pierced her curtains. Everyone flung on clothes and rushed outside. The hay bales in the big barn, stacked high with the latest crop from the summer harvest, were engulfed in a blaze originating from a pile of loose hay at their base. Smoke poured from under the eaves, and the glare from the flames danced around the farm buildings like Guy Faulks night.

We grabbed hoses, extinguishers, buckets – anything to help. Old Jim came staggering up from his cottage, having seen the light. We were lucky. The fire had only just started, and it was mainly the loose stuff that was burning. The tightly packed bales themselves did not catch immediately.

As we began to get on top of it, I looked around for the source – fury burning fiercer than the flames themselves. I could see no clue. But then, peering through the gloom to the far side of the land, I noticed a distant dark shape on the hillside. It was the small figure of someone struggling up the steepest slope on the fell.

'There!' I shouted, pointing. I commanded Jim and Annie, 'Finish the fire off!,' and ran for the buggy.

Lily beat me to it. She was racing for the near paddock, where Chardonnay lazed her privileged life. She whistled to the horse, leapt on bareback, and galloped full pelt for the looming hillside. She was able to go almost straight up, whereas I had to take the buggy on the roundabout route, to cut the intruder off higher up. As the machine bounced and slithered up the narrow rabbit run between the gorse patches, I watched her. She and Shard ran down the figure staggering up the steep slope, and as they caught up, Lily stuck out a leg and caught the fugitive full in the back, a rugby kick that was worth six points. Whoever it was went flat into a gorse thicket.

I skidded to a stop beside them, jumped off, and with my good arm hauled the whimpering form out of the bush. It was a youth, wearing dark clothes and a woollen hat, gorse pricks bleeding down his cheeks. He was collapsing at the knees, but I hauled him to his feet.

'I know you,' I said, peering through the semi-dark at his streaked and blubbering face. 'You're Frank Arnshaw's boy. What the fuck d'you think you're doing?'

The lad was barely seventeen years old, son of the village garage owner. A harmless, simple youth, pupil at the local school, often seen dawdling around the playground and the pond with his mates.

'Well?' I repeated. 'Answer me!'

He could barely speak, blathering and stuttering between his sobs of terror. 'I didn't... I'm sorry... I couldn't...'

My anger erupted. I smacked him hard across the face, and grabbed his coat again. 'Who put you up to this? Who?'

I was about to throttle him, when Lilly put a gentle hand on my shoulder. 'Dad, let me. I know him.'

I pulled away, calming murderous thoughts. She held the boy with both hands.

'Was it you, Sean? Did you start the fire?'

He stared at her, eyes like a frightened frog's, blood streaks running down his forehead.

'Why? Why did you do it?'

He found his stammering Yorkshire voice. 'It were this bloke. He got talkin' to us in the café. He bought me and Colin doughnuts and... and...' He tailed off.

'And what? What did he do?'

'He were just chattin'. Askin' about the village and that. Said he were thinkin' of movin' here. And he asked about the farms around, and was there any for sale, or anything.'

103

'And?'

'Well... He were very friendly like, and it seemed strange.'

'Strange? Why?'

'Well, he weren't from these parts. He were quite well dressed. But he said he were lookin' for a nice farm to invest money in. And then he asked about yours.'

I intervened then. 'Ours? He knew about ours?'

The boy nodded, eyes glazed, waiting for another assault. 'He said he knew you. Said you'd cheated on him, and he wanted to get his own back.'

'Cheated on him? How?'

'Didn't say. Just said you owed him. Said you needed a lesson.' He snivelled, and brushed at his wounds with a sleeve. 'I thought it odd because I didn't think you were that sort. But then he... he...'

'He what?'

'He pulled out a pile of money, and waved it at us. Said he was offerin' five hundred pounds to someone who could do what he wanted.'

'Poison my water?'

'What? No...' His look of bewilderment was genuine.

'So, just set my hay barn on fire.'

His silence was answer enough. The night and the stars glowered at him. 'And you fell for it.'

He began weeping again. 'I'm sorry, Mr Oldfield. I didn't... I just... I'd been savin' for a new smart phone, and...'

'And you thought that it was worth going to prison for the sake of getting your Twitter messages.'

His eyed widened. 'I won't go to prison, will I?'

'You might well do, Sean. Depends.'

'On what?'

'How much you tell us. Who was this man? What was his name?'

He shook his head. 'I dunno. He never told us. He just... I mean, when I said I'd do it, he sent Colin off so he could just talk to me. He gave me two hundred right there, and said I'd have the rest when it was done.'

'How was he going to pay the rest?'

'He said he'd leave it for me somewhere. He'd send me a message on my phone once he knew your barn had burnt down.'

I gazed at him. He was too artless to be making it up. 'You're a silly boy, Sean.'

More nods. 'I'm sorry, Mr Oldfield. I just... I just...'

'You just thought it was easy money, and you'd get away with it. Well, let this be a lesson. You very rarely get away with doing bad things. They always catch up with you in the end. You're just lucky we killed the fire before it did real damage.'

He was crying like a six year-old caught scrumping apples. I hadn't the heart to punish him further.

'How did you get here?' I said. The village was a couple of miles off.

He pointed vaguely. 'Bike. I left it on the road.'

'Well, get straight home, and don't tell anyone about this. If you do, it'll get to the police, and then you're done for.'

He nodded. I stood aside, and he stumbled off along the hillside. He suddenly reminded me of other dark figures staggering along hillsides, far off in another land. And involved in a far more serious war.

Later, when we had doused the embers, cleaned ourselves up, and gone back to bed, I lay there staring up at the ancient beams in the ceiling. The spiders had weaved fishnets up there, but that was all right. The anger still smouldered inside me, but now it had condensed into a shape, like molten metal forged in the blacksmith's fire. It had to be utilised. Something had to be done with it, or it would just lie there, cooling until it was dead and rusting.

'Right, that's it,' I said. 'I'm going to London tomorrow.'

Annie was coming naked out of the bathroom, but for once it didn't divert me. 'To do what?' she said.

'To have it out with them. I'm not having any more of this nonsense.'

'What will you say?'

'I don't know. But believe me, it won't be friendly.'

She climbed into bed and cuddled up. 'You can't go accusing people like that without proof.'

'Proof? What proof do I need? Constant attempts to sabotage our business here. It's not the fairies doing it.'

'The lawyer said you should go to the police.'

'That was over the poisoning. If I get them in now, they'll want to know about the fire too, and then that lad's future will be wrecked.'

'You don't need to mention that we caught him.'

'Then I'd be breaking the law myself. Withholding evidence.' I sighed. 'This is all getting out of hand.'

She was doing naughty things under the sheets. 'Shall I come with you?'

I turned my head. 'Why would you want to do that?'

She pouted. 'Just to see where they work. See London again.'

'I'd rather do it on my own. You'd weaken me, being there.'

She stopped trying to seduce me. 'So you're going to just barge into their offices and threaten them with war? David and Goliath in the middle of London?'

'Well, I can't just ignore it, can I? What will they do next? I'll take my slingshot with me.'

'Just be careful you don't inflame the situation.'

'Hah! It can't be more inflammatory than burning down barns!'

She turned on her side without answering. I went to sleep with the smell of burnt hay still wafting round the house.

CHAPTER SEVENTEEN

toosday. 7.00. nise day. 17C. yestiday we had a fir in the hay barn. dad and mum and lily and jim put it out with lots of water. dad and lily cachd the man who did it. i know him from the vilige. i dont now why he did it. im glad it didn burn any of the animels. fire is ecsiting but dangerus. mis tomas my teecher says it wos the first thing that mad us difrent from the animels becos we cud cook and keep warm with it. but i think ther are uther things that make us difrent

On the train to London – no first-class ticket this time – I worked out my own Machiavellian plan. For once I barely noticed the passing landscapes. By the time we reached King's Cross I knew what I was going to do. I wasn't going to enter the lion's den. I needed to find their vulnerable point. Face their weakest combatant on neutral ground.

The son. He was my target.

Back in the roar and stink, I caught a taxi to the Dragonsmead offices. It was around half twelve when I arrived, perfect timing. I stationed myself across the road from the entrance, a little way down the street, half hidden behind a big pavement waste bin overflowing with disposable plastic, though how and where it was disposed I had no idea. The day was overcast. London was in one of its morose moods. Or perhaps it was just reflecting my own. The traffic passed in an unending chain link. Where the hell were they all going? I waited.

Sure enough, as one o'clock approached, the staff began to leave. Singly and in pairs. Secretaries, suited young men, portly middle-aged executives. Heading for the pubs and the fast-food takeaways. The city routine.

I waited for fifteen minutes, and was beginning to think that today was not to be the day, when I saw him. Martin Collins, accompanied by another of similar age and similar dark tailored suit. They were deep in conversation as they left the front door and walked smartly away from me down the street. How absorbed people were with their own preoccupations, and how disconnected most of those were.

I followed, on the far side, feeling like a character from a John le Carré novel. I wished I'd brought dark glasses, but perhaps that would have been overdoing it. We walked for five minutes - they talking all the way, me a cat prowling after pigeons. They came to a smart Italian restaurant - darkened window, elegant canopy, gold lettering - and went in. I waited opposite.

I gave them a few more minutes, time enough to get settled, then crossed the road and peered in through the window, shading my eyes against the reflection. I could dimly make out white table-cloths, nodding heads, side alcoves. I pushed open the door and entered.

An elderly Italian waiter greeted me – grey hair, white apron, and Mediterranean toothy smile. 'Si, signore?'

'Ah – it's all right. I've just come to give a message to someone here,' I said. 'Mr Collins – I think he's just arrived.'

'Ah, si signore,' and he obligingly lead the way to one of the alcoves.

It was large enough for four, but only Collins junior was there, with his colleague seated opposite. Wine glasses the size of saucepans already stood before them, with dark red alcohol a quarter of the way up. They looked up as I came to the end of the table.

'Roger!' Collins was suitably startled.

'Sorry to interrupt your lunch,' I said. 'But you and I need to talk.'

There was a five second pause as they both assessed the situation. Then he said to the other, 'Would you mind, Peter? I'll see you back at the office.'

The man called Peter pushed aside his napkin and his wine glass. 'Seems important. I'll leave you to it.' He got up, gave me a wan smile, and left.

Collins waved a hand to his seat, and I sat. Soft cushions, low lights, lush potted plants. If the food wasn't good the ambience made up for it. He said, 'I can give you a few minutes. Julia's joining me soon for a quick lunch.'

'That's all I need.' I picked up the other's abandoned wine glass. 'Shame to waste this. Mind if I have it? I could do with a drink.'

He didn't move or speak as I drank. Not a bad chianti. I felt marginally more confident. I put down the glass, and leaned forward with my arm on the table. Around us the discreet murmur of business people talking, and the clink of cutlery. The movers and shakers at the trough.

'I just want to know, Martin, what it is you hope to achieve by it all.'

A shadow of puzzlement crossed his face. 'All what?'

'You know what.'

'No, I don't.'

'Straying sheep, poisoned waters, burning barns. That's what.'

'Poisoned waters?'

'Yes. Officially diagnosed. I lost cows and milk production. And I nearly lost my winter hay store to arson.'

Silence. He looked bemused. 'All since we saw you?'

The first spark of doubt hit me. Either he was a Oscar winning actor, or he was genuinely mystified.

'Perhaps your father kept you in the dark.'

'My father? He would never instigate that sort of thing.'

'Really?'

'Of course not. He may play tough, but that would be madness. If anything like that got out the whole company would be in trouble.'

I studied his face for signs of guile, but there were none. 'Then who else could it be? This is a concerted assault to put me out of business.'

Before he could answer, a waiter arrived with pen and pad at the ready. 'Would you like to order, signori?' Waiters never wait for the end of conversations.

Collins waved a hand. 'Oh, I'll just have a Caesar salad, please.' He looked at me. 'Do you want something to eat?'

'No, thanks. I'll stick with the wine.'

The waiter left. He stared into his own glass for a long moment. I didn't interrupt his thoughts.

Eventually he picked up a fork and dawdled with it on the table-cloth. 'The only thing I can think of is that it's...'

'Who?'

'Blackall Quarries.'

'The present owners?'

'Yes.'

'Why? Why them?'

'They're in trouble. They're desperate for the sale to go through. They've been wanting to get rid of Stainbridge since they stopped working it.'

I struggled to understand.

He went on. 'They're an old-fashioned outfit, badly managed. They have other interests, but they've been going downhill for a while.'

'Who owns them?'

'They're publicly quoted, but the family's a majority share-holder.'

'What family?'

He didn't answer immediately. Just played with his fork. He was too good-looking for his own good. 'I'm not saying it's them, Roger. I don't want to start a false hare. But I can't think who else would be so involved. This deal is their life saver.'

'How much are we talking?'

'Several million. We're still haggling. We're debating whether we should just buy the quarry, or take over the whole company, with all their other assets.'

'Other assets?"

'They own digs and land ventures around the country. None as profitable as they used to be. We're assessing it all. It's quite a long process. But none of it will be viable without Stainbridge.'

'How would this guerrilla warfare help their cause?'

He shrugged. 'Force your hand. Make things so difficult for you that you throw in the towel.' The blue eyes gazed directly. 'You see, everything depends on how negotiations go with you. The sale could be crucial to saving their company.'

I sat back. 'Jesus!' Took another sip of the chianti. I felt like draining a bottle. 'So who are they, this family?'

'The Blackalls. They're based in Manchester. Originated in the slums there, but fought their way up in the world.'

I remembered what Fred the vet had said about Lancashire number plates at Faulkner's farm. 'Why don't they do what you want to do? Mine Stainbridge further?'

'They haven't the resources. Haven't the skills. Modern mining is a scientific business. They're too old-fashioned.'

The warm air wafted around us. The scent of Italian cooking was beginning to make me hungry. 'What are they like, the family? How many are there?'

'The third generation are running it now. Two brothers and a sister. But they're a rough lot. Their father and grandfather built the business years ago. Real old quarrymen. But the present lot haven't got any of their nouse or integrity. We're finding them quite hard to deal with.'

'I'm not surprised – if these are the sort of tactics they're using.'

He looked around. 'Look, er... This is very awkward. I, um...'

The waiter arrived with his salad. It looked good, but wasn't my kind of food. He stuck his fork in and messed with a lettuce leaf. Then he looked back at me. 'Of course it would all go away if you accepted our offer.'

I gave him my cat stare back. 'No way, Martin. I don't give in to tactics like that. If they want a war, they'll get one.'

He nodded. I felt sorry for him. He was born into a situation not of his choosing. A prince in the royal court who could never escape.

At that moment his girlfriend arrived at the table. She looked very different from her appearance at the castle. Smart work suit, hair swept back, immaculate makeup. A more formidable look - the professional uniform. She raised her eyebrows at my presence.

'Oh, Roger. I didn't expect to see you here.'

'Neither did I,' said Collins. 'He's a surprise visitor.' He moved to the side and indicated the place next to him. 'Sit down, darling.'

111

She sat beside him and gave me a smart smile. City princess to country peasant. 'Well, it's nice to see you again.'

I half smiled back. He said, 'Roger's having trouble with sabotage attempts. We think it might be the Blackall lot.'

'Sabotage?'

'Assaults on his animals and his buildings.'

Her perfect face clouded. 'How awful!' She threw him a look. 'Not you, is it? Not your father?'

He darkened. 'That's what Roger assumed. I'm surprised you would do so as well.'

She raised a cynical geometric eyebrow. 'Well, we all know what he's capable of.'

'Nothing as crude as that.'

'No. And you're certainly not capable.' There was an edge to her voice. He threw her a look. I sensed a tension, like rough fabric on sensitive skin.

The waiter arrived. 'I'll have the same,' she said, pointing at his salad. 'And a glass of pinot grigio.' Then the grey eyes turned back to me. 'So are you here to negotiate terms?'

'No.'

'Good. You can't surrender to that sort of thing.'

He glowered at her. 'Hey!'

'Well, of course he can't, Martin. I've no axe to grind in this, but those are the kind of tactics that give business a bad name.'

'Thank you,' I said.

She examined me with her head on one side. 'However, if I were you, I'd screw them all for as much as I could get, and go and live in luxury somewhere sunny.'

I smiled. 'That's what everyone says. But you're not me.'

'No.'

'And, looking at you now, I doubt you'd do that either.'

She straightened the collar on her already straight jacket. 'No, but then... Well, we are all different species.' To Martin, 'Aren't we, darling?'

He was finally eating some of his greenery. 'Roger and we live in different worlds, if that's what you mean.'

'Yes. That's it. Different worlds.'

I didn't disagree. I sat back in my cushions, watching her with curiosity. She had two sides, like an actor switching roles. I said, 'So you work in this world too?'

'I'm in investment banking. In the City.'

'Do you like it – your different world?'

She smiled back at me. 'I love it.'

I was intrigued. 'What do you love?'

'The challenge. The drama. The excitement.' She waved a long-fingered hand at the restaurant. 'The pleasures.'

I nodded. Part of me understood. 'Not so different to mine then really. Just less dangerous.'

'Oh – don't you believe it. This is just as much a jungle. We may not lose arms, but we can lose minds.'

I glanced at Martin. He was staring at the table-cloth. There was something incompatible about the pair.

'And do you love your world, Martin?' I said.

She answered for him. 'Martin tolerates it. He'd really rather be sailing the world in his boat.'

'Boat?'

'Mhm. Exploring ocean depths.'

That seemed incongruous, given the circumstances. 'That's interesting,' I said. 'A different kind of challenge.'

He said, 'Yes. Very different.' His face flickered with the reflection from his wine glass. 'Fascinating.'

'So were you brought up with boats?'

'No. I took to them later. Or rather took to the seas.' His expression was suddenly hard. 'They hold the clues.'

'To what?'

He didn't answer immediately. She said, 'Global warming.'

'Oh, that.'

His look was steelier still. 'You don't believe it?'

'I know it may be yet another thing that farmers have to worry about.'

'Yes, it is.'

It was evidently something that moved him more than limestone quarries. I said, 'Then why don't you go after it?'

The steel melted, and he almost visibly deflated. He shrugged dismissively. 'We can't always do what we want, can we? People who can follow their dream are lucky.'

She stroked his arm as if to a cat. 'Poor Martin. Daddy bullies him as much as everyone else. But at least it means he earns enough to follow his dream one day.'

He gently shrugged her hand off, and threw me a wry look.

I drained my balloon of a glass. 'Well, I won't disturb your lunch any further. I'll be getting back to my world.' I eased myself out of the alcove. 'But global warming apart, if my farm is being threatened by your quarry owners, you'd better warn them not to muckspread with me or I'll come after them. Jungle warfare.'

I could almost feel their eyes pricking me between the shoulder blades, as I walked from the restaurant.

CHAPTER EIGHTEEN

wedsday. 11.43. sratus clowdy. 16C. dad gon to lundun tiday. lily at scool. grampa poorly with a cold. mum bizy. im bord. not many birds to wotch tiday. orl my favrit composers died before 40 mozart and gurshwin and mendelsun. i might die before 40 too. lily says orl genyuss die erly and that means im a genyus too. i don't know wot a genyus is

I broke out into bright daylight again. I took a deep breath, and then wished I hadn't. The traffic fumes stung like mustard gas. It wasn't long past one o'clock. The meeting had been brief, so now I had time to put the second part of my plan into action. I started walking. It was over a mile to where I wanted to go, but the skies had cleared, and if I went through the parks I could clear my head too.

As I marched, I called a number on my phone. I got instant contact with Reception. 'Hello – my name is Roger Oldfield. I'm a North Yorkshire committee member. Is Terence Lacey in the building? Oh, well when he gets back from lunch, can you tell him that I'm on my way to the offices and I'd like to grab a few minutes of his time. It's rather urgent. Thank you.'

The National Farmers Union HQ is based in Smith Square, in the heart of Westminster. I knew it well. Committee meetings there were like a batch of poultry fighting over a bucket of feed. Local representatives from all over the country used their trips to London to squabble, lobby, crusade, and booze. They ranged from raddled old-timers from the fierce crags of Wales and Cumberland, to lofty gentlemen farmers from Sussex and East Anglia, to young upstart reformers from the plush pastures of Dorset and Hereford. Put all their heads together and you'd solve the world's feeding problems in a pig's snort. But that was the problem. Getting their heads together.

I strode back through Mayfair to Hyde Park, then across to St

James's Park and through to Whitehall. The gardeners' efforts flaunted themselves with florid magnificence. Buildings soared. History and Empire and the wealth of civilisation swirled around me, and despite my wariness of cities I had to feel awed. Sheep may have been the foundation of much of it, but now this was the foundation of modern man's existence.

I reached the NFU building and entered. The usual security measures. I said to the girl at the desk. 'Roger Oldfield. I've come to see Terence Lacey. Is he back from lunch yet?'

She gave me a nice smile. City receptionists all have the same smile, but that's all right - a smile is better than a smack any day. 'He came back with a takeaway ten minutes ago, Mr Oldfield. I told him you were coming. He has an appointment at two, but he said he could see you if you arrived before then.'

I looked at my watch. It was twenty to two. She pointed me the way. The lift was busy so I sprinted up the stairs to his floor, found his door, knocked and went in.

Terence was a senior administrator in the Hill Farming department. I knew him quite well, after many meetings there. He was a southerner, but easygoing and a frank talker. I got straight to the point.

'Thanks for seeing me, Terry. Do you know about my issue with a railway going through my land?'

He was chewing on a huge baguette stuffed with enough protein and greenery to feed my family for a week. A big polystyrene cup of coke sat in front of him, amongst a bushland of paperwork. 'I saw the briefing, Roger. What's happening with it?'

I filled him in with a synopsis of the story.

He ruminated whilst ruminating. 'That all sounds very tortuous. Extremely contentious. Highly controversial.' Loved long words, did Terence.

'I need to get to the powers that be in Westminster. They're the only ones who can put a stop to the whole shenanigans. I was hoping you could point me in the right direction.'

He pondered more, and chewed more. 'The Minister for the

Environment is probably your best bet on an issue like this. We can lobby him once your appeal gets official, but meanwhile...'

'Meanwhile, I'd like to try and do something while I'm down in London. And before my farm gets wiped out by a tsunami or a nuclear bombing raid.'

'Well, you won't be able to get to him personally. In any case he won't have much to do with it directly. It'll be his minions in one of the departments.' He took a long swig through the straw at his liquid sugar whilst contemplating. He was overweight already, but that was his problem. 'Tell you what. I know a chap there who might know something about it. Quite senior. A deputy director. I could give him a call.'

'Thank you, Terry, that would be good.'

He ploughed through his papers to find the internal government number, and put through a call. Managed to get past the secretaries and spoke. 'Geoffrey, this is Terry Lacey at the NFU. I've got a chap here – Yorkshire farmer – has a problem with a compulsory purchase order. Industry wanting to run freight trains through his valley. The Stainbridge Quarry issue. The company has lodged planning applications and are putting pressure on. The locals are up in arms, and the whole thing is threatening to explode into a global confrontation. Do you know anything about it?'

He took another bite of his baguette whilst listening. Then spoke through his mouthful. 'Yep. That's it. Well, I've got the fellow here. Know him well – he's on one of the local committees. Good sort. He's only in London for the day. Any chance you could see him for a few minutes?' He listened more whilst pulling faces at me. 'Yes, he understands that. But he'd just like to tell someone his side of the story, other than just the usual... Yes. Yes. No. Yes. That's good of you, Geoffrey. I'll send him along.' And he put the phone down.

'He'll see me?' I said.

'Yes. Warns that it's strictly unofficial, and he can't bypass the proper channels and all that nonsense. But, as you and I know, the proper channels can sometimes be channeled improperly with a little bit of help from one's friends. Anyway, it can't do any harm.'

'I'm very grateful. Thanks a million.'

'If you trot along now, you should catch him. It's in the Home Office Building – ten minutes walk. His name's Geoffrey Tennant.'

As I've said, it's who you know.

Tennant was a different kettle of fish to Terry Lacey. Classic civil servant – about my age, tall, eagle beaked, thick hair already tinged with academic grey at the edges. He had the same expression they all have – impregnable authority hiding the fact that they can do bugger all about anything really.

He shook my hand, waved me to an uncomfortable looking chair in his plate-glass plastic bowl office with views over the squat rooftops of officialdom, and went back to his desk. Not a paper on it – just a phone and a pad and a photo of his picture book family.

'This is my assistant, Jeremy Dickson.' He indicated a young man standing to one side, who looked younger than Lily, but with a neater haircut. He must have left university with dazzling degrees. He smiled and shook hands, and sat back in a corner.

His boss unfolded himself into his big leather swivel chair. 'So, Roger – may I call you that – I know a little about your case. Why don't you fill me in on the detail?'

I gave him the full gory drama, with embellishments. When I had done, he sat for a long time swivelling from side to side, tapping a fountain pen on the desk top. I didn't know they still had those. Then he looked down his hawk's nose at me.

'You haven't lodged a statutory objection yet?'

'No. I want to resolve it before we get to that.'

A dry smile. 'Probably wise. But that means persuading the applicants that their case is a hopeless one.'

'Yes. Which is why I need your advice.'

More pen tapping. 'The thing is, you see, Roger, you're up against conflicting interests here. If it was just up to us at Environment, then we could scupper it for all the obvious reasons. Even though we are keen to promote stone as an environmentally sound building material. However, we have to negotiate with our colleagues at the Department for Business and Industry, who have to negotiate with their colleagues at the Department for Transport, who have to negotiate with the Cabinet Office, who have to negotiate back to us. And then we all have to negotiate with every other Tom, Dick and Harry who want to have a say in the matter.'

'Yes,' I said. 'But after you've all done negotiating, who in fact has the final say?'

'Well, if we can't agree amongst ourselves – which I have to say from experience is an unlikely outcome – then there would have to be an official inquiry set up. A legal panel of experts appointed, who would take representations from all the departments and all the interested parties, and who would eventually come to a decision on the matter.'

I sighed. This was getting me nowhere. 'Yes, I understand that, Mr Tennant. But what I'm really asking is, who do you think would win in the end?'

He threw me an ironic smile. 'Ah well, that's a million dollar question.'

'Yes, but you're used to dealing in million dollar questions, aren't you?'

He had the grace to chuckle. 'Ah, but the more millions involved, the trickier it is answering the questions.' Then he pursed his lips and threw a look at his assistant. 'There is another factor, which you're probably unaware of, and which may not be in your favour.'

'What's that?'

'This is in strict confidence, you understand. Off the record, hypothetical, pure hearsay.'

Why can't these people talk straight? 'What?'

'As you probably know, the government has committed to improving things up in your distant part of the world. Devolved powers, boost to industry, improved transport links – and so on.'

'Yes.'

'One of the major challenges is to provide better rail links from east to west across the north of England. Liverpool across to Sheffield, Carlisle across to Newcastle – that sort of thing. The

Pennines, down the spine of the country, have always been a big obstacle. There aren't many obvious routes through them.'

A heavy weight descended on my chest, like the water tank coming down all that time ago. I waited, frozen.

'I know that the Transport people are viewing this as a possible trial run for a rail route through your area. If the quarry line goes through, then at some time in the future it could be used as an opportunity to simply extend it westwards, make it a double track line, and turn it into an official National Rail route.'

I could swear that even the clock on Big Ben up the road, had stopped turning. After a century or so of silence, I said, 'So what you're saying is that we'd have major building works, and then passenger trains running through our farm every few minutes.'

He had the grace to look awkward. 'Well, not every few minutes, but... And of course it wouldn't happen for some years.'

Years or hours – what did it matter? This would be hanging over our heads for evermore.

He was watching me with something like sympathy on his vulture's face. 'Not what you wanted to hear. I'm sorry.'

I sat motionless. It wasn't his fault. He was stuck in the whole vast conspiracy of what was called progress. Finally I said, 'That's all right, Mr Tennant. You're probably used to living with trains rattling around you all day. We're not. I don't quite know what we're going to do about this.'

He glanced again at his young assistant, who hadn't said a word so far. 'What do you think, Jeremy?'

The kid uncrossed his legs, and smoothed the crease left on his trousers. 'Well, it would seem that the best thing Mr Oldfield can do, is to win the initial battle against the quarry line before it gets to inquiry stage. Then everything else falls away.'

'But how do I do that? I'm not going to use their tactics.'

They both looked blank. I looked back. We all looked at each other.

Eventually the older man said, 'Public opinion. That's what decides in the end. Everyone is scared of public opinion. Get all the

120

locals to start shouting. Get Madonna, and Spiderman, and George Clooney, and Prince William, and the Pope to make statements supporting you, and you'll probably win.'

'Thanks,' I said. 'Very helpful.' And I left.

CHAPTER NINETEEN

fryday. 9.46. 16C. in bed, got grampas cold. dont lik it. mum mad me drink horid stuf. lily werking for exams. i lisend to mi gurshwin

Stress is like chilli pepper. It either chokes you or fires you up. Challenge is either a depressant or an aphrodisiac. It's why some people fight to the death, and some say fuck it, life's too short anyway. I'd known a number of people who'd fought to the death. I'd almost been there myself. But this was a different kind of death.

I rang home and told Annie I wouldn't be home until tomorrow. She didn't ask why, just if I was all right.

'Yes,' I said. 'Terrific.'

'Be sure you're back for Danny's birthday.'

I took the train to Manchester. Not a spectacular journey. The Midlands countryside doesn't compare with the Dales. On the way I reflected how ironic it was that I could dash around the country by train, yet here I was trying to stop the things. By the time I got there it was evening. I had never been to Manchester, even though it was half the distance of London from home. I found a cab at the station rank, and said to the coloured cabbie through the window, 'I want a nice comfortable hotel that's not too big, and not too noisy, and not too modern.'

He threw me a dour look. 'Not fussy then.' He had the flat Lancashire accent, so different from the earthy Yorkshire one. 'Get in.' His cab smelt of old potato chips and cigarettes.

He drove through the sprawling city, once the heart of the Industrial Revolution. A weird mixture of Victorian Gothic and shiny modern – like outsize diamonds scattered across a pebble beach. He dropped me at a big brick building that looked like a converted warehouse. But inside was nice. Eccentric but nice. Rough stone walls and marble fireplaces and quirky decor. The food wasn't bad either. I didn't have Lily for company this time, but I ate a big dinner, drank too much wine, and slept like a drugged squirrel. I dreamed I was on board a steam train ploughing through floods and fires and packed flocks of sheep, whilst I wrestled with the controls.

Next morning, after a stylish breakfast with more fruit than I'd eaten in a month, I took another taxi. It had been a simple matter to discover where the company was based. It was a good twenty minutes drive through dreary suburbs before we reached the place, and my nerves got tighter with every one of them. It was a huge sprawling yard on the outskirts of the city. Above the open gateway hung a rusting sign – Blackall Quarries. Inside the littered space, the size of a football pitch, stood great piles of assorted stone slabs, paving stones, tiles, rocks, chippings, gravel, and for all I could tell, human bones. A heavy lifting tractor was piling stuff into a big truck, causing a thunderous crash with every bucket load. This was the mess that eventually created every pristine building.

The air was biting as I paid the cabbie off, and made my cautious way across the mud and the debris to the sagging brick office block standing to one side. A large silver-grey Mercedes with tinted windows and a Lancashire number plate stood beside it. The car had seen better days, like the building.

A sign on the main door said 'Enquiries'. I opened it and went in.

An old boy wearing a streaky beard and overalls stood behind the counter. Wooden shelves with nothing on them ranked behind him, and worn catalogues that looked as if they were printed during the last century lay about. He was barely big enough to see over the top, but he was on the phone and waving a pencil. He paused in his conversation as I entered, and registered vague surprise at seeing anyone that time of the morning.

'Is the boss here?' I asked.

'Which boss?'

'Any boss.'

'Mr Blackall senior's up in his office.' He nodded towards the wooden staircase.

'Yes, that's who I want.' And I headed for the stairs before he could say any more.

On the first floor was a corridor with a series of offices and store rooms. I found a door with a frosted glass panel on which was written 'Administration'. Voices came from within. I put on my casual face, knocked and went in.

A heavy set fellow wearing a rumpled check shirt and loose tie sat behind a big old desk. He had a half-beard, and was probably in his mid-fifties, but looked older. A woman stood beside him. The pair were bent over some papers. They stopped talking and looked up.

I closed the door behind me, and stood there looking at them. They looked back. The room was stuffy with cigarette smoke and the fumes from an old-fashioned oil stove standing in one corner. It augmented an iron radiator that should have been good enough to heat a concert hall, but evidently wasn't.

'Know who I am?' I said. There's no point trying to go places incognito when you've only got one arm.

The man flickered minutely at the empty sleeve, and back. Of course he knew. 'What d'you want?' He had that same flat pungent accent.

'I thought we should have a talk.' I stepped forward and sat uninvited in the chair in front of the desk. Attack is the best form of defence. They both stared at me like frogs watching a snake. 'Is this your secretary?' I said. 'You may not want her in on this.'

'It's my sister. She's a director of the company.'

'Oh, good. The more directors the merrier.'

She straightened up. A buxom woman with streaked blonde hair and mauve lipstick. Wearing a tight skirt and tighter blouse, both of which were at full stretch. She'd probably been quite attractive once, and was hanging on bravely. She too was fighting the new way of the world. We all have our battles.

'So?' said her brother.

'So...' I hadn't really planned what I was going to say. You can't plan these things until you know what you're walking into. 'This business of the Stainbridge quarry.'

'What about it?'

'I'm intrigued. Why are you so desperate to sell it?'

He stubbed out his cigarette in an ash tray. The smoke still curled to the low ceiling. 'That's our business.'

'Oh, but it's mine as well. It's very much mine.'

'Why?'

'Well, it's affecting my own business quite a lot. As I'm sure you're aware.'

They briefly looked at each other, then the woman walked to the side, pulled up another chair and sat. She didn't say anything – just looked at me, holding her cigarette like a small hand grenade.

I went on. 'I ask again. Why are you so very desperate to sell?'

Then she spoke. 'It's a lot of money.' Her voice was a lot softer on the ear than his.

'So it must be valuable then.'

'Yes.'

'Because of the stone still there.'

'Yes.'

'Then why aren't you mining it?'

He said, 'Why are you askin'?'

'I'm interested. Humour me.'

'It's too difficult. Too deep.'

'But you're mining experts. You've been mining for generations.'

His glower was not pleasant. Like a burnt loaf left too long in the oven. 'It's a major operation. Needs big machines, big resources. We've got too much else on our hands.'

'Yes, so I gather. Like saving the company.'

The loaf blackened further. 'Look 'ere, Mr, um...'

'Oldfield.'

'Oldfield, yeh. How we run our business is our business. Why are you pryin'?

'As I said, it's my business too.'

'Well, let me ask you a question.'

'Go ahead.'

'Why are you so agin sellin?'

How could I explain to people like this? We were from different worlds, we spoke different languages. 'Let's just say that I'm the custodian of a unique corner of England that needs to be preserved before it vanishes for ever.' The fumes from the stove clogged my nostrils. I loosened my tie. 'Oh, and you see, when people try to poison my herds and burn down my barns, it makes me more bloody minded than ever.'

They were silent - whether embarrassed, awed, or bemused I couldn't say, but the silence told me it had to be them. Eventually the woman said, 'We're talking millions of pounds at stake here. Enough to do all sorts for your place. What difference is one little railway line going to make?'

'It's not just one little railway line though, is it?' I said. 'Once that's in, they'll follow it with double tracks, mainline trains, station stops, and possibly the Great Wall of China.'

They didn't show surprise. They knew about the possibilities. I went on. 'The thing is this. You also have something to be proud of. Something that's been in your family for generations. Something your ancestors have built up over decades, and provides valuable resources for the region. Why are you letting it go?' I paused. 'Well?'

'There isn't the call for stone and gravel now,' he said.

'Yes, there is.'

If his frown had got any deeper his eyebrows would have met his chin. 'Are you tellin' me my job?'

'Yes. I've looked at the stats. There's huge demand for building material. That's why Dragonsmead want your quarry. If they're that keen, there must be a helluva lot of value there.' He shifted in his seat. I looked from one to the other. 'So is it just ignorance or laziness that stops you?'

He cracked then. He pushed back his chair and got up. He was a big man. He pointed a stained finger across the desk at me. 'You mind yer own fuckin' business! I dunno what you hope to achieve by bargin' in here, but it's not gonna work, Mr bloody one-arm Oldfield. Now get out of my office before I fuckin' throw you out!'

I smiled and got up. It had been a very short exchange for such a long journey, but I'd found what I needed to know. I knew who I was dealing with.

'Yes, I'll leave now,' I said, and went to the door. I turned and said, 'But I warn you. If there are any more incidents at my farm, I'll be back with a shot gun.'

The train journey back home was a tortuous one involving two changes. I didn't get home until late evening. I could see why east-west lines were needed.

CHAPTER TWENTY

fryday. 7.27. nice day. 21C. mi cold is neerly beter. dad cam bac from lundun. he had his cros look on but evry bodys at home tiday lily too. it is mi birf day so we wil hav a speshil diner with al my no 1 best things. ther was my presints beside the bed wen i wok up. they wer a fab car book from lily and a big caby net from mumdad with a lot of drores made of plas tic for my colecshin wich i always wonted. you can put nams on evry drore and ther are big drores for big stuf and smal drores for smal stuf. its alredy nirly ful.

i have to stop colecting things

I had to delay the Land Tribunal inquest. The odds were stacked against us. We needed time to find a strategy. I called in the police to investigate the water poisoning business, although I didn't tell them I knew who was behind it.

A couple of them rolled up in a squad car one misty morning. They were from the Barnard Castle station, and I knew the senior of the pair. He was a seasoned sergeant who'd been around for years and knew every farmer, shop-keeper, and tramp in the county. The kid with him was new to the job.

Trigger and I met them in the yard, as they were getting out of the car.

'Hello, Jack,' I said. 'Thanks for coming.'

'Any excuse to get out of the station, Roger,' he said, round red face glowing with either health or whiskey, I wasn't sure which. 'What's goin' on 'ere then? You got a war on your hands?'

'Something like that. Our water was poisoned a couple of weeks ago. Had to be deliberate.'

Trigger was sniffing at the young cop's trousers. The youth looked apprehensive. 'Here, Trigger,' I said. To the boy, 'He won't bite. Not unless you're a sheep thief.'

He smiled feebly. Jack said, 'Why've you taken so long to report it?'

'We weren't sure what it was. Had to wait for the lab report.' It was a poor excuse, but he accepted it.

'Any idea who might have done it?'

'Not sure. But you may know there's some pressure on for us to allow a rail track through the farm.'

He nodded. 'Heard about that. You think it's connected?'

'Well, it's an odd coincidence.'

'Mm.' He gazed around the yard. His eyes rested on the hay barn at the far end, where the timbers still showed signs of the fire. He evidently knew about that too. 'What happened there?'

'Yes. We had a fire there too. Caught it in time, and can't prove it was deliberate, but...' I shrugged. I wasn't going to rat on the idiot boy from the village. Hopefully they wouldn't enquire too much into that.

'Well,' he said, turning to his companion, 'this 'ere's Ronnie. He's learnin' the Sherlock Holmes business, so you'd better show us your water tanks, and how you think they were sabotaged.'

I waved at the hillsides. 'We think they must have poisoned the becks that feed the tanks. They wouldn't have dared come down to the fields.'

He grunted. 'Ay well, a bit of exercise won't do us harm. Ronnie, get the boots from the car.' Police in those parts came equipped for all terrains and all weathers.

The three of us and Trigger crossed the river and examined the troughs on that side. A pointless exercise, as I knew it would be, but I explained how the fell water was piped into them - a miraculous labour-saving supply. Then we climbed up the lower slopes. Sergeant Jack puffed as he rolled his way up, and the lad slipped and stumbled. He wasn't a country boy, that was obvious. I took them to the likely places, where the water trickled down over the rocks, and the midges hovered above. Trigger drank from the clear stream, as he always did.

The bobbies made a show of searching the ground for footprints

129

and clues, but of course found nothing.

'Well, this don't tell us much.' Jack wiped his ruddy features with his sleeve, and stood looking out over the valley. 'So where's this rail line goin' to run?'

'It isn't, Jack. Not if I have anything to do with it.' I pointed. 'But the proposed route is along those pastures there.'

They both gazed down across the fields, lying like beautiful women waiting to be taken. The heather was in full bloom, and the scent tinged the air. He muttered, 'I can see why you don't want it. Bootiful place you've got here.'

'Yes.'

'So what d'you want us to do 'ere?' He was looking at me out of the corner of his eye. He wasn't stupid.

I gave him a half smile. 'I'd like you to record this as an official police investigation, Jack. You don't need to do much work on it, as long as it's on the books. I want to delay the rail inquiry as long as possible, you see. Give us time to marshal our forces, if you know what I mean.'

He nodded. 'Ar. I reckon we could do that.' Looked at his companion. 'What d'you think, Ronnie? Serious business this. Might have to bring in Scotland Yard, eh?'

The lad looked bewildered. He didn't know quite what was going on. Jack clapped him on the shoulder. 'Never mind. You'll learn. We all help each other in these parts. Let's get back to the car.' Real old-school copper was Jack.

We headed back down the hill, which was easier going, but easier falling also .

They made it safely. 'Coming in for a coffee or something?' I said, when we reached the yard.

He shook his head. 'Love to, Roger, but I've got the boss breathin' down my neck right now. Town's full of travellers and bikies this time of year, and the crime rate's summat rotten. Thank yerself lucky you've just got polluted water to worry about.'

'Okay. Thanks for coming.'

I hoped they wouldn't be back in the future for something more serious.

That weekend I called a council of war meeting. All the gang. Myself and Annie and Lily and Danny and my father, and even old Jim. Six of us round the kitchen table, not counting Trigger and the cats. A coffee pot and mugs stood around. Outside it was blowing a gale, and the rain was starting. The land was reminding us that it too could rebel.

'We have to decide what we're going to do, people,' I said. 'We're up against big forces. Big business, big government, big crooks, big money. They're determined to have their rail line, and possibly a major rail link in the future. The question is, do we make this a Waterloo, or do we give in, grab the money, and learn to live with trains thundering through night and day?'

'Or grab the money and sell,' said my father.

Why did everyone wish to play devil's advocate with me? I threw him a look that would have stopped a tank. 'We're not doing that. You wouldn't have done that.'

He shrugged, his gnarled face like a sculptured ape's. 'Probably not.'

There was silence. The Aga hissed, the roof creaked in the wind, the cats purred.

Eventually Annie raised her head. 'If we fight them, what are the options?'

'We can use all the official routes – appeals, objections, petitions – but from what I've gleaned in London they'd probably fail. We could conduct a protest campaign, get the local press and media on our side, and raise the whole county against it, which might perhaps delay things further, but could fail also. Or we could pray to God to work one of his miracles.'

'Allah would be better,' said Danny. 'He can do miracles.'

'She,' said Lily.

He didn't hear. He was chewing on a large bun. 'You could put some bones there.'

We all looked at him.

131

He went on with his mouth full. 'They were building a road somewhere, and they found some bones in the ground. It was a Saxon village, so they had to stop.'

Lily said, 'That's it, Dad. Plant some cow bones on the route and say they're dinosaur fossils.'

Ah, the carefree days of youth. 'Can we be serious, please,' I said 'This is our future we're talking about here.' I looked at my father. 'What do you say, Dad?'

He was glowering at the colours on Annie's table cloth. 'Wish I was younger,' he said. 'I'd show those buggers a thing or two.'

'I've no doubt you would. But what should *we* do?'

'Well... it's not for me to say. I had a son to hand things over to, but you... Well, Lily's not going to be running the farm, is she? Nor Danny. What will you do with it when you want to retire?'

'That's a long way off, Dad.'

'Mebbe. But we're talking long term, aren't we?' He sniffed. 'I dunno. It's not up to me. It's up to you young ones.'

I turned to Lily. 'What do you think, Lily?'

She shrugged. 'Not my decision either, Dad. I'd hate to see the valley go, but as I'll never want to be a farmer I don't really have a say.'

'Of course you have a say. What about breeding your horses?'

'I can do that anywhere. Probably better places than the Yorkshire moors.'

'But you'll inherit it. Railway lines and all. Sheep and cattle and Danny probably. It's your legacy.'

She glanced at Danny, and her eyes were suddenly filled with tears. 'Oh god, Dad, I don't know. I can't answer.'

I relented. 'All right.' I looked at Jim, who was hunched at the end of the table like an old gnome who'd found himself in the wrong place. 'Jim – do you have an opinion on this? You've been on the farm longer than any of us.'

'Not fer me to say either, boss. I dunno how to deal with these people.' He blinked bleary eyes at his coffee mug as if it was a crystal ball. 'I don't understand how the world works now. But if you want someone to ride shotgun with you, I'm up fer that.'

I smiled. 'Well, that's good to know.' Then I turned to Annie. I'd left her to last. She was the one who would decide in the end, one way or the other. 'Annie?'

She had been listening, playing with her china cup in its saucer. Didn't go for mugs, Annie. 'Perhaps I should discuss it with you later,' she said.

'No. We're all in this together. Say what you're thinking.'

'I'm not sure what I'm thinking.'

'Yes, you are. You're always sure.'

She took a deep breath. 'Well... it seems to me that most people have to make big decisions at some time or another. Most people change direction in mid-life. Whether it's jobs, places, marriages — countries even. Maybe this is the fates telling us something.' She held my gaze, unflinching.

I stared back. 'You want to change job, marriage, and country?'

She smiled. 'Of course not. But maybe lifestyle. I mean, this is an opportunity that will never come our way again. Enough money to do whatever we want. I know the farm and farming has been everything for you, all your life. But maybe it's a chance to experience a different life.'

My mind was blank. I couldn't really comprehend what she was saying. It was a suggestion that had never entered my consciousness, like a proposal to live on the moon. Five pairs of eyes were on me. Six including Trigger.

'You mean sell up and become an estate agent, or a stockbroker?'

Her eyes flashed. She never rose to my sarcasms. 'Don't be silly. But you've got lots of skills. There is so much you've never experienced. The farm's been your whole world, but it's not all there is.'

'Is it a different life you want?'

She hesitated. 'What I don't want is a long protracted warfare. What I don't want is more dangerous incidents. What I don't want is for it to bankrupt us. What will happen if we don't accept their offer and they win the legal battle? Will the offer then be withdrawn?'

It was something that had occurred to me, but I hadn't wished to contemplate.

'So we surrender?' I said. 'We lose everything we've fought for here, and let this little piece of England fade away like all the rest.'

'It won't be the end of it. Just a line through the Van Gogh.'

I snapped. It happens sometimes. Banged my fist on the table, shaking the coffee mugs, and got up. 'Right! Plough it all up! Build railways and stations and factories all over it! Turn it into Danny's safari park, and let the whole world in!'

And I stormed out into the wind and the rain. I knew I was being childish, but I couldn't help it.

That night, when both I and the weather had calmed down, and we lay in bed, I turned to her and said, 'Would you like a different life? Have you had enough of the farm? Do you want a real change?'

She didn't answer for a long moment. 'I love it here, Roger. We've been happy here, and it's been great for the kids. But sometimes fate forces your hand. I wouldn't object to a change. I've no idea to what, but there are other things in life than weather and sheep dung.'

'Such as?'

She pulled the cover up to her chin. 'I said, I don't know. But there are valleys elsewhere that aren't so challenging. There are farms all over the world that need help or advice. And there are places to experience. Places in England, places abroad...'

'I've been abroad. It wasn't fun.'

'You know what I mean. There's Rome, and Barcelona, and Australia, and the Mississippi, and the Sahara Desert...' She tailed off.

'That's a good idea. Let's start a sheep farm in the Sahara Desert.'

She didn't smile. 'You know what I'm saying.'

I thought I did, but I wasn't sure. Such visions were far outside my horizon. We were still nowhere clearer as to what to do.

CHAPTER TWENTY ONE

satiday. 21.10. nite. 14C. 2 polis men cam yestiday. they cam in a bmw x5
polis car wich is turbo chargd. they went with dad to find who put stuf in the
water. i wonted to go too but I wasn't alowd. we had a famly meting in the
kichin to tok abot wot to do with the farm and the rail way. dad had a tan
trum. i dont lik orl this abowt the rail way its too long. its hirting mumdad.
its just a rail way

The media finally got hold of the story. The local paper had already printed an innocuous piece about the rail plan, but now the Yorkshire Post got whiff of the controversy. A far more influential paper, with national coverage. A reporter rang me one morning, and asked if she could visit with a photographer. Much as I hate being photographed, I knew this could help our campaign, so I consented.

They turned up on a sparkling autumnal afternoon. A dapper young woman in jeans and sweater, already equipped with walking boots, and an equally youthful male photographer with hair longer than hers and a camera that could probably have photographed the galaxy. Is it me, or is the world now being run by university graduates?

She sent the lad off to photograph the farm, while she talked to Annie and me in the drawing room. It was chilly in there, as we hadn't lit any fires and were saving on the oil-fired central heating, but it was more appropriate than the turmoil in the kitchen. I told her as much as I could of the whole saga, without slandering anyone in particular. As I got further into the melodrama, with embellishments from Annie, the girl's expression gradually changed from polite editorial interest to sparkling-eyed enthralment. She sensed a story.

She asked a lot of subsidiary questions, wanted to know more about the farm's history, and showed particular interest in both my crippling incident, and Danny's place in the household. I said they had nothing to do with the rail controversy, but she seemed to think otherwise, and was quite persistent. She also wanted to know about my army experiences, and whether that affected my way of dealing with the problem. I started to get angry, but managed to control myself. She was just doing her job, as we all were. And maybe she had a point. In the final analysis, everything affects everything else. Homily for the day.

She got the photographer to take shots of all the family in various combinations, and in evocative locations around the farm. It took longer than I expected, and I chafed at the lost hours.

When the pair had left, late in the day, we all looked at each other.

'What have we started?' said Annie.

'It depends what slant she puts on it,' I said.

'What's a slant?' said Danny

'It's whether you make it a monster story, a detective story, or a friendly bedtime story,' said Lily.

'I think it should be a murder mystry,' said Danny.

I murmured to Annie, 'I hope it doesn't end that way.'

That weekend they published the article. A double page spread, with photographs of the valley in all its glory, and of myself in closeup with cropped arm showing, and of the four of us together with Trigger at our feet.

The headline read:

BRAVE YORKSHIRE FAMILY FIGHT GOVERNMENT AND INDUSTRY TO SAVE THEIR ANCIENT FARMLAND.

The article described in vivid detail the beauties of the landscape, the 'heroic' nature of the family and its misfortunes, and the ruthless tactics of the titanic forces ranged against it. It was a tear-jerker to make the world weep. Over the weekend we got a dozen phone calls from friends and acquaintances, ranging from the sympathetic 'how shocking', to the 'grab the dosh and run' variety.

Soon after, I received another call from the media.

'Is that Roger Oldfield?' asked the female voice. 'This the BBC in

London. I have Jeremy Onoja, Current Affairs producer, who would like to speak with you.'

My heart jumped a series of beats. I should have anticipated it. The BBC loves a social controversy.

A deep voice, somewhere around bottom C, came on. 'Ah, Roger, we're very interested in your campaign to prevent people running rail lines through your land. It's an intriguing story. We haven't decided yet which of our current affairs programs might be most suitable to air this on, but would you be willing to come to London for an interview on your situation?'

At this rate I might as well set up home in London. 'Um... well, I've already lost a lot of time over the issue. Couldn't it be recorded at one of your regional studios closer to home?'

'Well, we see this as something having national impact, Roger. The small man against the big corporations, commerce versus the environment – that sort of thing. And most of that is handled in London. Of course we can always do your appearance remotely, but it's so much better when we can have you face-to-face in the studio. We'd pay your expenses of course.'

First-class train and five-star hotel, I was tempted to ask? 'Well, I er... I'll have to see when I can get away from the farm. When would you want me?'

'Sometime next week if possible. We'd like to catch the story while it's hot. We'd get a local film crew to come and film your farm in action - perhaps capture your animals and family members in their natural habitat – ha, ha. But we'd really like to see you personally in our studios here in London.'

'Well, give me twenty-four hours and I'll see what I can arrange.'

I was in two minds. Actually three minds. First, it was of course the kind of publicity that could sway the whole campaign, as everyone kept telling me. Second, however, it would be making me a celebrity victim figure, which was the last thing I wanted. And third, I was already far behind with the farm after all the diversions.

I took my morning coffee out to the porch to think about it. It was always a good place to think. The views to the high fells were uplifting, the farm smells were calming, the distance from office and household gadgetry was liberating. I sat and sipped, and pondered.

Annie came out, also cup in hand.

'Are you going to do it?' she asked. She knew my fear of exposing myself.

'I ought to. It's a great opportunity to publicise the whole bloody affair. But the idea of going on national television is... well, you know.'

'Yes.' She smiled. 'I know.'

She sat beside me on the bench. We were both quiet for several moments. The she said, 'Why don't I do it?'

I looked at her in surprise. 'You?'

'Yes.'

I took a minute to assimilate the idea. 'Would you... I mean, would you want to?'

'I wouldn't mind. I'm not so scared of cameras as you are. I know all the arguments. And there are other factors.'

'Such as?'

'I'd stay calmer than you. I'm prettier than you. And I wouldn't be trying to hide my stump under the table during it all.'

I had to acknowledge all three of those.

'Of course,' she went on thoughtfully, 'having a woman trespassing on such male territory might be against us, and your stump might elicit a lot more sympathy than my hairdo.'

My instinct, however, had immediately responded to the suggestion. I'm a great believer in instinct. It's usually more reliable than trying to intellectually analyse situations.

'Actually,' I said, 'we might get more sympathy if it's a woman who's being threatened by evil conspiracies. The MeToo crowd will be all on your side.'

She raised a dry eyebrow. 'This isn't about sexual harassment.'

'Well, there's no harm in associating with it.'

She went quiet then, staring out across the fields. Sunlight shivered across her face. 'Yes,' she said. 'I think I could do it. And I'd like to have a bit of time in London.'

Ah, I thought. There was an ulterior motive. Even so, I was warming to the idea. 'Well, as long as you did the business, and as long as you didn't get seduced by some smart BBC presenter, and as long as you didn't bankrupt us with thousand-pound opera tickets, I'd have no objection. I know you'd wow them all much better than I could.

She sipped her coffee, and sat back, a look of calm anticipation on her lovely face.

The BBC went for the idea with surprising enthusiasm. But then they're very female orientated these days.

The next day a two-man camera crew from Leeds rolled up. They went round the farm filming all of us, and every activity from Trigger rounding up stray sheep to the flies buzzing round the slurry pit. I tolerated them, Annie and Lily preened for them, Jim and Father hid from them, and Danny dogged them. They were there for several hours, and when I asked when it would be showing in the cinemas, they laughed and said we'd get an invitation to the Oscars.

The following Monday, I drove Annie to the station, briefing her all the way on what the interview might bring up. She had on a nifty black trouser suit with a red silk blouse underneath, which I hardly remembered seeing before. You might have thought she was a company executive going for a top-level board meeting. I said it was too chic for a beleaguered farmer's wife, but she said, don't worry, she had a more feminine dress in her overnight case for the interview. This was just in case she had a chance to pick up a rich businessman on the train. Not in BBC cattle class, I said. No, she said, but she was going to upgrade to first class. I wondered if I was doing the right thing letting her go. She kissed me and waved through the window as the train pulled out of the station. I suddenly felt abandoned, as I stood on the platform watching it disappear.

We all watched that evening when the program was aired. It was one of those current affairs shows that come on after the news, and involve shiny tables and swirling backdrops and scarily confident and knowledgeable hosts. This one had a well-known male presenter, wearing a suit and a bright tie that I swear was fluorescent. The first item was an interview with a politician who was vainly trying to defend a proposed new bill to outlaw gender discrimination in advertising. He tied himself in knots trying to explain how you could promote tampons without being gender specific.

Then it was our turn. The presenter sat in the middle. On one side sat Annie, looking adorable in a floral dress with her hair swept demurely back, and on the other sat Martin Collins.

I was taken aback. It hadn't occurred to me that they would bring in the enemy, but of course I should have known. He looked calm, debonair, and friendly.

The interviewer opened up. 'And now we come to an item that has hit the headlines recently, and which highlights one of the greatly relevant issues facing us today, in this advanced and overcrowded island. What matters most? The development of the economy and living conditions, or the preservation of our landscape and heritage.'

He went on to introduce the pair at the table, and explained briefly the circumstances of the controversy, whilst showing the film clips of the family, and of work going on around the farm. I was thankful the crew had come when the weather was fine, and not when it was playing at Wuthering Heights. Then he talked to Annie, and she explained the history of the place, the great challenges the family had suffered over three generations to preserve such a unique part of Britain's topography and heritage, together with a potted version of my grandfather's appeal to me on his deathbed. It was heart-warming.

Next, Collins took the floor. He gave a persuasive account of the extraordinary lengths the company went to in order to protect environments, compensate communities, and improve local amenities, and ended with an equally heart-warming description of the great benefits to society and to conservation presented by the supply of fabulous Yorkshire limestone.

Finally, a junior minister came on via external link, and was quizzed about the government's attitude towards such schemes. He managed to sound hugely concerned and sympathetic on the whole issue, without saying anything meaningful whatsoever.

When it was over, I reckoned we'd come out just about evens. I asked the others what they thought.

'You should have done it,' said my father. 'Annie's too sentimental.'

'Nonsense,' said Lily. 'That's what the public loves.'

'They didn't show my insect collection,' said Danny.

Annie rang late from her hotel. I had started to worry, not hearing from her. But I assumed she'd been dining out with some of the BBC's hotshots. A chance to flirt with city slickers – she'd enjoy that.

But her voice was subdued. 'How do you think it went?' she said.

'Great,' I said. 'You were brilliant.'

'I'm not sure it will make much difference.'

'Oh, I think it will. Although I didn't anticipate them bringing on Martin Collins.'

'Neither did I. I only found out an hour before the interview.'

'You should have rung to tell me.'

I sensed her hesitation. 'I didn't... I was too occupied with makeup and briefings, and so on. And I wasn't... I needed time to think out how to respond to him being there.'

'How was he?'

'What do you mean?'

'Towards you?'

A slight pause. 'Very friendly. Didn't try to intimidate me or anything.'

'They were clever not to bring on daddy. He'd have intimidated everyone.'

'Yes.' Another hesitation. 'Um... sweetheart, would you mind if I stayed another night tomorrow?'

'In London? Why?'

'It's so rare I get the chance. I'd love to do gallery or something today, and maybe a show tonight. The hotel's not too expensive.'

I could hardly refuse. I'd be in her good books for days. 'Yes, of course. Enjoy yourself.'

CHAPTER TWENTY TWO

wedsday. 6.32. ciris clowds. 16C. mum not heer dad owt so got my own brekfist. tost and weetbix and choclit and milk. we al wotchd mum on tely last nite. she is famus. she takd abot the farm and they showd us al doing stuf and triger geting the sheep and me in the kichin. but they didn show my insec colecshin. dad ancshus last nite. he dusnt lik it wen mum not heer

Maybe I should have known. Maybe I should have guessed what would happen. There was always a secret corner of Annie that she kept from me. I knew that a part of her pined for that other side of life. That she missed the swirl and buzz of city life, the stimulus of culture and smart people. Dr Johnson was ever whispering in her ear. But we both avoided the subject since there was little to be done about it. It was a world that I had forsaken because my own world was so dominating.

When she got back from the capital she was different somehow. Bright and cheerful, and happy about the interview. And enthusiastic about her day in town and her evening at the National Theatre. But there was a reticence there. Something else that I couldn't define. The simmer of a burning coal that hadn't yet died.

Two days went by. The aftermath of the TV interview rumbled on. Various journalists and feature writers rang, and I dealt with them as briefly and as politely as I could. The interest gradually faded, and we were almost back to normal again.

Except that Annie was not normal. Her tension and false cheerfulness began to get on my nerves. I knew something was wrong, but we could not talk about it. We went about our work with dull faces, which broke into false cheerfulness as we passed each other, like polite strangers on the village footpath. I wanted to challenge her, force her to talk, but since I had no conception of what could be troubling her I did not know how to broach the matter. We were aliens in our own home.

Then on the third night, after a day of virtually no discourse, she went to bed before me, and was asleep before I came up. Whether genuine or faked, I couldn't tell. I undressed in the dark, and slipped like an unwelcome intruder beneath the sheets.

In the middle of the night I woke, and sensed that something was wrong. I realised that she wasn't there beside me. I noticed there was a light on in the bathroom, and I got up to see what had happened. I found her in her dressing gown, leaning on the basin with tears rolling down her face.

'What is it? What's the matter?'

She turned, and put her arms round my neck, and buried her face in my shoulder. 'I'm sorry,' she said. 'I'm so sorry.'

'What? What is it?'

She didn't reply. I pulled away, and stared into her tear-stained face. 'For Christ's sake – what is it?'

'Martin. Martin Collins...'

'What about him?'

'I went to bed with him.'

My body froze, my mind shut down.

She was going on. 'I didn't... we didn't go all the way. I stopped. I couldn't do it. But... but I nearly did.' Her tears were falling onto the collar of her dressing gown. 'I'm sorry. I'm so sorry.'

I found a voice. 'How? Why?'

'I just... I got carried away. It was London, the interview, the contrast with everything here. I got seduced. Not so much by him. By the experience.' She wiped a sleeve over her cheek. 'I was just stupid.'

Through the fog of my incomprehension, I bizarrely felt relief that at least it was now out in the open.

They had gone out to dinner together after leaving the studio. He told her that Julia had broken up with him. He wasn't dynamic enough for her, she'd said. He was in quite a bad way over it. Then, over filet steak and burgundy, they talked about London and books

143

and theatre and a lot of other stuff. They hardly mentioned the farm and the railway. He took her to her hotel and kissed her goodnight. The next day, he met her after lunch and they went to the Tate Modern. They nearly got thrown out for laughing so much at all the nonsense that called itself art. That evening they went to the National Theatre and saw a production of Oscar Wilde's *The Constant Wife*. Very ironic. Then he took her for another drunken and expensive dinner somewhere, and they ended up back at her hotel again. This time he didn't kiss her goodnight, but came in with her.

Even though the mystery of her behaviour was now solved, I could not process it. My mind was in a quicksand. He was almost a decade younger than her, and from another world. She had never strayed in all our twenty odd years of marriage, and neither had I. We had been enough for each other, I thought. Except we weren't.

The subconscious works in strange ways. I understood how it had happened. She'd been drunk on wine, on freedom, on the city - but however much I told myself it was understandable, it was a unique situation that didn't have any real significance - my heart could not accept it. I could not envisage the alternative seductions to which she was so vulnerable. The incompatible pulls of urban sophistication and rural simplicity that so unbalanced her. We are all slaves to our natures.

A black fog descended, and I could no longer think rationally. I went about the daily routine automatically, but I could not look at her, or talk to her, or think about her. I became a walking ghost.

Annie herself, after that terrible night, accepted my state of mind, and went quietly about her own business without referring to it again. The rest of the family knew that something had happened, but didn't ask. They were becoming immune to crises. The one thing farming teaches you is patience. Everything passes, the pendulum swings, nature will reassert itself.

Except that this time it didn't have time to reassert itself. Impatience asserted itself instead.

We received notice that an official Land Tribunal inquiry into the rail scheme and the compulsory purchase order had been brought forward, and we had fifteen days to prepare our case. Someone had been pulling strings. The two worlds were about to collide.

CHAPTER TWENTY THREE

toosday. 21.46. nite time. 14C. cant sleep. sumthing rong. dad sad face mum quiit lily quiit evrybody quiit. wen peeple are quiit it meens they are lowd inside. play my mozart 21. cant sleep

We didn't know why they had suddenly decided to accelerate the process. Possibly the BBC program had scared the pants off them, and they wanted to get the thing over before the opposition gathered momentum. Procedures were waved through, red tape was circumvented, the police investigation into the water poisoning was brushed aside. When officialdom wants to, it can move fast.

I was glad I had done so much preparation in advance. But even so I was floundering in the face of the bureaucratic juggernaut. We had considerable forces on our side, but bringing them all together and organising them for a coherent presentation was going to be a business. I felt I was fighting single-handedly, and it wasn't a joke.

Then I received a call. I recognised the Old Etonian voice immediately. Sir Peter, the baronet, himself.

'Good morning, Roger. I hear the official inquiry has been set.'

'Yes, Sir Peter. It has rather taken us by surprise.'

'Well, don't worry. You've talked to our legal chap, Jeremy Driscoll - we'll get him to handle it all. He's red hot at this sort of thing. And don't fret about the cost. We'll handle his charges. This is something that affects the whole county. And I'll do what I can in Westminster.' The waves of privileged confidence filtered over the airways like a balm.

'Thank you, Sir Peter. I couldn't have fought this without your help.'

'Well, we all need friends at such times. Don't worry, we'll get the bastards.'

The weight on my shoulders lifted slightly. I no longer felt it was a lone battle against superior forces.

They had stipulated that the hearing would be held at York. This would allow any of the officials to come and inspect the site if they so wished. It was a relief to me. I had no desire to make another London trip. I spent the next days in a fever of preparation. At least I had something to distract me from more personal matters.

Annie quietly handled the secretarial work. She lost weight. We barely spoke. Even the hens knew something was wrong.

The inquiry was held in a courtroom of the York Magistrates Court, a great ugly Gothic brick building across the city from the towering Minster, by contrast surely one of the most magnificent creations of man. I went on my own since the witness numbers were limited, and in any case there was little point other family members being there.

I met the London lawyer for the first time in the reception area beforehand. He had travelled up by train the night before, together with a female assistant exuding efficiency. He was stout, she was stout, and they each carried stout brief cases stuffed with papers. Together with my own files, we had enough paperwork to keep the whole civil service busy. Driscoll, surprisingly, was a short, tubby little man with a receding forehead and large ears. Quite unlike the urbane image I'd conjured from his telephone voice. But then voices often don't go with faces.

'Just let me handle our side of things,' he said. 'I'll call on you at the right strategic moments. The other side have brought in some heavyweight legal brains, but we've got enough ammunition here to make the panel think twice about waving the whole thing through on a nod and a wink.'

'Who will be deciding it?' I said.

'Oh, there'll be a senior lawyer chairing, and big guns from the various ministries. I'm not sure yet who's on which side, and who's been subjugated to what pressures, but we'll soon winkle them out.' He patted my good arm reassuringly. 'Don't worry. We'll give as good as we get.' I suppose it's a lawyer's job to be reassuring.

We entered the wide courtroom to find it already thronged with a dozen suited people of various ages, sizes, and sexes. Files and reports littered the tables amongst the water jugs. A screen and business projector stood at one side. The murmur of conversation sounded like the rumble of tanks lining up for battle.

I loosened my tie, and sat next to Driscoll who was already laying out papers in front of him. The woman sank her large backside on his other side. Thankfully, none of the Collins family were there, which saved me having to commit homicide there in the courtroom. Just James Garrick, their hill-walking project manager, who gave me a brief nod and then buried himself in a sheaf of papers. He was evidently going to be the company's chief spokesman.

A nondescript man eventually emerged from the throng, introduced himself with a slight Essex accent as the QC chair of the proceedings, and called the meeting to order with the air of a school prefect. Everyone who wasn't already sitting did so, and he gestured round the tables introducing them all. An array of official faces that for some reason made me think of Animal Farm.

The following hours passed me by in a rising tsunami of talk. Countless paragraphs from obscure reports, endless industrial and transport statistics, convoluted legislative regulations, statements from apparently interested parties who I'd never heard of. Phrases such as 'statutory obligations', 'relevant authorities', 'admissible objections', 'environmental constraints' flew about the room like a swarm of bureaucratic butterflies.

My representative showed himself to be a brilliant contestant. He had all the information I had provided at his finger-tips, plus a good amount of his own. Every argument produced a documented counter argument, every petition provoked an opposing petition, every statement inspired a contesting statement. He painted the valley as a unique fairy-tale site that was one of the glories of Britain's heritage, which, along with the Crown Jewels and Nelson's Column, should never be vandalised. The screen was regularly consulted with projected graphs and illustrations. I was occasionally called upon to clarify some detail about the farm and its procedures. Garrick did the same for Dragonsmead. At one point the entire BBC interview was shown, to a scattering of nods, whether applauding Annie or the other side I couldn't tell. Lunch was a simple offering of sandwiches and soft drinks, miraculously appearing from nowhere, and passed around with scarcely an interruption to the debate.

Finally, at around five in the evening, we seemed to have reached some sort of conclusion. I, who had had the least to say, appeared to be the most exhausted person present. The chairman thanked everyone profusely for their attendance, stated that the panel would announce their verdict shortly, and declared the show over. Several people took their leave of me, shaking hands as if to an old friend, and wished me luck. I left with Driscoll and his partner, none the wiser as to what the outcome might be.

The pair took their leave on the pavement outside. 'I'll let you know as soon as we hear anything,' he said. 'You can never tell from people's reactions at these things which side they'll come down on. I'm often surprised at who votes which way. But we're in with a good chance.'

I had to accept that as the best reassurance I could get. I went home to further days of fraught suspense, numbed farm routines, and wordless relations between my wife and I.

Three days later, Driscoll rang. His voice was low. 'I'm afraid we lost.'

I waited, unable to comprehend.

'They've given the go-ahead for the compulsory purchase order, and for the rail track.'

I could hear in the background the distant sound of traffic outside his office. I still said nothing.

He went on. 'I'm very sorry. You'll be compensated to the agricultural value of the amount of land taken. But I'm afraid it was a battle of the ministries, and aesthetics lost to economics.'

Compensated? What did that mean? He rumbled on, explaining the small print in the decision, but I scarcely heard. Not for the first time in my life, the world had closed its doors on me.

CHAPTER TWENTY FOUR

toosday. 19.08. cold tiday. 12C. my speshil scool day tiday. we did memry gams and i finishd making mi engin. i like speshil scool days its boring at home evrybody sad. nobody plays with me not even grampa much. lily wating for her exam risults she stays owt most days. dad dusnt do lesons much with me. he says we mite hav to hav the rail way. mumdad dont talk. i wish i cud do sum thing but i don't under stand enuf abowt every thing. it seems ezy to me but its not

I climbed Shere Fell alone, except for Trigger and my shotgun. I only had the shotgun for rabbits and game birds. Now I actually considered using it for something else. I had lost my farm, my wife, my self. Life had become death.

When I reached the summit, I sat on the rock and contemplated the valley below. I could almost see the great scar that would now disfigure its face. I imagined the feelings of a woman whose beauty had been destroyed by a jealous lover. Would she wish to live?

I looked at Trigger. He was sitting, watching me with untypical concern in his eyes. He knew something was wrong. A cloud spread across the face of the sun as if to confirm the fact.

It was only because of Lily and Danny that I stopped. You think that you live for yourself, but you don't. You think that your vocation is everything, but it's not. In the end you live for other people.

I watched a flock of wood pigeons skimming the valley like dive bombers in formation. I watched the farm slowly unfolding its business. It was oblivious. It had no interest in human affairs.

We stayed up there for an untold length of time, until the dark and the cold sent us back down again.

Three weeks after the hearing, a letter landed from the Department of Transport. A bland, impersonal letter, cold as vanilla ice cream. It stated that a team would be arriving the following month to prepare for the commencement of works. They required access to the farm, and would be creating fences on either side of the proposed rail route. They would of course provide gates and crossing points for my animals – thoughtful of them. They would also need to create a new entrance to the land from the lane. It would be at the point the rail line would be exiting. This would then follow the lane and the roads all the way to the Darlington main line link.

Annie touched my arm in the first physical contact we'd had for weeks. Her eyes were lined and sad. 'I'm so sorry,' she said.

I was too distracted with my own feelings about it all to wonder about hers, but I knew she was in as great a turmoil as I was. I sat and stared at the letter for the next decade or so. I was too numb to react.

However others did react.

I never had much to do with the social media. I watched half the world wandering around like sleepwalkers, hypnotised by their smart phones, and I always wondered whether they actually had lives outside the small screen. Of course I used emails, but Twitter and Facebook were just icons cluttering my computer as far as I was concerned. Life on earth, it seemed to me, was slowly evolving into a never-ending picture show.

Now, however, I became aware that these weird means of communication might have occasional use. It was Lily who alerted us to what was happening. Lily had got great results in her final exams, without apparently actually studying hard at anything, but she wasn't interested in using them to go the traditional professions route. Never did things the orthodox way, Lily. She got herself a job as stable girl at a nearby racehorse stud, and spent her days happily exercising horses and shovelling manure. She came home one afternoon, sweat-stained and happy, and said, 'Have you seen what's happening on Twitter, Dad, Mum? There's a ton of stuff going round about the railway. People are getting very worked up.'

She showed us some of the postings, and the statistics. Then we went to Facebook and Instagram. The same thing was happening. The messages were from farmers, business owners, nature conservationists, school children, ordinary householders. They ranged from alarmed to indignant to unprintable.

I was impressed. 'Well, that's all very heart warming,' I said. 'But it's too late now. The decision's been made.'

I hadn't reckoned with the bloody-minded Yorkshire mentality. I hadn't reckoned with the human proclivity for going to war, even though I had known it myself once.

The day came when the works team was due to arrive. I was up at dawn, had a quick breakfast, and went out as always to start the rounds, a grim weight on my heart. It was an ordinary day - no biblical portents manifesting. The skies were clear, so there was little chance of the weather coming to my rescue. The animals were calm, the hills still soared in sublime majesty.

But as soon as I got out into the yard, I became aware of a cacophony of noise coming from the direction of the lane. It sounded as if the circus had come to town.

I muttered to Trigger, 'They can't have come this early, surely?'

Trigger wagged his tail, thinking hopefully it was something he could chase. We strode out towards the sounds, meeting Jim on the way, who had also heard. The three of us reached the boundary wall. There were about a hundred people in the lane, accompanied by tractors, trucks, jeeps, and even a towering combine harvester. The road was blocked in both directions, and what looked like a riotous street party was in progress. Chatter, laughter, music, and the clinking of beer bottles and coffee mugs. Someone had even erected a banner: NO RALES IN THE DALES

A cheer went up as we appeared. We gazed over the wall in astonishment. People waved, and reached across to shake my hand. A girl thrust a leaflet into it.

Then my neighbour, Mike Foster came forward, wide grin splitting his wide face. 'Beats Greenham Common, eh?'

'Did you organise this?' I asked.

'Nah. It organised itself. Word went round the airways what was happening, the start date was common knowledge, and people decided to take the law into their own hands.' He gazed round at the noisy mob. 'You'd think they were celebrating Dunkirk.'

I wasn't sure how to react. 'Well, it's a great show of support,' I said. 'But what happens when the work force shows up?'

'They'll stop 'em. They've blocked the road. You won't get construction workers wanting to clash with protestors. It's not in their job description.'

'And when the police show up?'

'They won't bring the riot squad in yet. It's a peaceful protest. As long as they let any normal traffic through, I doubt the police will do much.' He cocked an eyebrow. 'Don't think you get much normal traffic past here anyway.'

I couldn't assimilate what was happening. 'Then what happens tomorrow, and the next day, and the next?'

'I dunno.' He turned and pointed up the lane to the far side of the crowd, where a group of people were gathered, conversing more seriously. 'But they seem to be forming some sort of committee.' He shouted above the noise. 'Vincent! Audrey!' And beckoned.

Two people detached themselves, and pushed their way through the carnival towards us.

Mike said, 'This is Roger Oldfield. Tell him what you're thinking.'

They were a youngish couple, anoraked and gum-booted, exuding educated diligence. The man wore glasses and an intellectual expression. 'Nice to meet you,' he said. 'I'm a teacher at Barnard Castle school.'

'Ah,' I said. 'I'm an ex-pupil.'

'Oh, good. Don't think I taught you.' He had a sense of humour, so that was all right. He indicated his companion. 'And this is Audrey Manning. She's with me on the local Protection of Rural England committee.'

I gave her a wave. We were like neighbours chatting over the garden fence.

He gestured at the crowd. 'This is a gratifying response. We didn't

153

know how many would come.'

'Did you have something to do with it?' I asked.

'A bit. But most have just turned up of their own volition. That's terrific, and with this turnout we can probably stop anything happening today.'

'Then what?'

He hesitated, and looked at the young woman. 'Yes,' he said. 'The problem is how to do so long term.'

She had that intense stone-jawed expression that said, I'm on the side of every social issue going, and don't you mess with me. She spoke. 'We think we need to organise this properly. We know quite a lot of local activists, and we'd like to form a committee, and establish a proper roster of protestors, who can provide continuing obstructions and road blocks to prevent these bloody people from doing their thing.' She was enjoying the prospect of battle.

'I'm very grateful for your support,' I said. 'But unfortunately, their thing has the backing of the law. What will you do if the other side calls up the cops in force?'

She brushed it aside. 'Oh, we have experience of all that. We helped Sir Peter Coverley in his campaign to stop a road through his estate.'

'Ah,' I said. Something I understood. 'Did he persuade you to help me?'

'Let's say he had words with our chairman,' she said, with a half-smile. 'Anyway, we know how to organise things, so that any violent clashes with the authorities will attract publicity that would give them serious indigestion.'

I had always wondered how these protests arose. It was a mysterious side of human activity that was foreign to me.

Her companion spoke. 'The thing is, this could be a long campaign. We have dedicated people who are prepared to sit it out, but they will need your help.'

'Anything we can do.'

'Just basics. They'd bring their own shelters and creature comforts. But a continuing supply of refreshments and hot drinks would be good. And any farm machinery that can help with roadblocks and so on.'

I had no idea how many bylaws and criminal codes I'd be breaching, but I was past caring. I looked at Jim beside me. He was glowering at the scene with a bemused expression. 'What do you think, Jim?'

He sniffed. 'Well, my grampa fought in the trenches, boss, so I reckon I could carry on the tradition.'

Well, if this was going to turn into a world war, who was I to stop it?

There was the sound of disturbance from down the lane. Shouts and jeers and the revving of engines.

'Sounds like the enemy are arriving,' said Mike Foster.

We all moved in that direction, us on one side of the wall, them on the other. The farm entrance was behind us, and the top gate to the lane was several hundred yards up the hillside. We came to where the altercation was happening. A small convoy of trucks and work tractors had arrived on the narrow lane, and had come up against the combine harvester and crowd of gesticulating protestors. Shouts, boos, and insults filled the air, with the suspicion of the odd missile. The convoy poised for a long moment, engines revving, yellow helmeted faces staring. The choice was plough into the crowd and cause a massacre, or retreat in ignominy. Deciding that discretion was the better part of valour, the vehicles started to reverse chaotically back up the lane again, accompanied by jeers and cheers from the mob. The sun brightened at that moment, evidently wanting to join in.

'Round one to us,' said Mike.

Later that day, the young couple came to the farmhouse door to talk with us. We sat around the kitchen table, me and Annie and my father, with the pair sitting opposite. Autumn was threatening to turn into winter, and the aga was going full blast. The latest generation of farm kittens were prowling about. I really ought to do something about them.

'Well, we've got a committee together,' said the young man with earnest brusqueness. 'And we've organised a roster – six hours on, six hours off. There's a good pool of volunteers. The problem is going to be if the police turn up in large numbers, but that will be their last resort.' His classroom eyes peered behind his specs. 'They'll try and coerce you first. Threaten you with proceedings unless you call the resistance off. Blocking a public highway, impeding official procedures, that sort of nonsense. You must simply say, it's nothing to do with you, and you have no influence over it.'

'What about night times?' said Annie.

'Yes, that might become a problem,' said the woman. Her campaign cheeks were glowing. 'We have to be able to open the lane as it's a public thoroughfare, and they may eventually attempt a nocturnal raid. We'll try and keep a skeleton guard there at nights, if you don't mind them camping in your field. They can give warning, and we'll have emergency barriers ready to bar the route when it happens.' She looked at me. 'Have you any farm implements we can use as roadblocks?'

My father waved a finger at me. He had come alive with the whole business. 'There's that old baler behind the cow shed. And the trailer we never use, with flat tyres.'

'Perfect,' she said. 'If anyone asks, we'll say we rescued them from disuse. You had no knowledge of it.'

'We've already alerted the local press,' said her colleague. 'The bigger the confrontation, the more they'll be interested. And if we can get the TV cameras along, even better. The more publicity we can get, the harder their job will be. You've no idea how many people there are who love a fight like this.'

It was the High Command planning the defence of the realm. I stared at the table top.

'Are you all right, Mr Oldfield?' the woman asked.

I rubbed my forehead. No, I wasn't all right, but what could I say? 'It's just... I'm very grateful for all that you're doing. I just didn't expect this kind of conflict on my doorstep.'

Her expression softened as much as it was capable. 'We realise it's

156

a huge disruption for you. But if you want to stop this bloody thing, then it's the only way. It's the future of the valley, isn't it?'

I hoped the valley would be suitably grateful. We talked some more high strategy, and they returned to their army camp.

The fuzz arrived next day. It was the same couple – my old friend Sergeant Jack and his young sidekick, Ronnie. They rolled up looking disgruntled, having been forced to drive the long way round to avoid the road blocks.

Jack puffed as he climbed out of their police SUV. 'Bloody 'ell, Roger! What are you doin'? We've got headquarters breathin' fire and brimstone. My chief has ordered me to come and put the thumbscrews on you.'

I put on my innocent face. Overnight I had come to appreciate the situation, and I was warming to the fight. I dreamed I was on the walls of Stalingrad. 'Nothing to do with me, Jack. It's the conservation lot. They're up in arms.'

His red face glowed redder. 'Don't gimme that! They wouldn't be doin' it without your sayso.'

'No, I promise you. We were waiting for the construction gang to turn up yesterday, but this lot beat them to it. They were here in force before the sun was up.'

'Well, they're breakin' every rule in the book! Obstructing a public highway, obstructing legal proceedings, obstructing bloody Magna Carta for all I know.'

'Talk to them, Jack. They're the ones doing the obstructing.'

He puffed. 'Fat lot of good that will do. I know these people. Don't give a damn about the regulations. Well, they'll be obstructing Her Majesty's armed forces if they're not careful.'

'Oh, come on. It'll never get to that. Imagine the headlines.'

'I am doin'. Long-serving police sergeant sacked for not upholdin' the law.'

I shrugged. 'I'll give you a job on the farm. Level crossing manager. Anyway, I thought you were on my side.'

He pouted. 'Well, mebbe I am at heart, but you can't fight the law,

Roger. You can't fight the whole bloomin' London establishment.'

'Public opinion can. That's what this is.'

He snorted. 'Public opinion, my arse! The public don't give a shit about landscapes. This is all your lefties jumpin' on one of their bandwagons.'

'You have a cynical opinion of human nature, Jack. People care more than you think. They like to know their landscapes are there, even though most of them only see them on the telly.' I had the feeling I was arguing against myself, but that was no bad thing.

He sighed. 'Ay well, whatever. What am I going to tell my chief?'

I glanced at his young companion, who was listening with a dumb expression on his face. 'Tell him you and your friend here did the full Charge of the Light Brigade, but you were overwhelmed by superior forces. I'll back you up.'

He gave another big sigh, looked around the yard, then up at the sky. 'Nice day. Got a bottle open by any chance?'

It's no wonder the public love our British police.

CHAPTER TWENTY FIVE

thirsday. 11.56. ciris clowds. 16C. swifts and swalows al gon to africa. very

ecsiting yestiday. lots of peepl cam to stop the rail way. they made a lot of nois

and wen the rail way peepl cam they fritind them away. then the polis cam

and tokd to dad but they cudnt stop the peepl. mum takin me to see them

tiday. mumdad mor hapy now. me too

It went on for days, and the days turned into weeks. The spirit of battle never dimmed their will. The protestors camped there night and day in all weathers, and never seemed to waver. Vincent and Audrey organised the roster with precise efficiency. The police came and went, officials tried to negotiate, the trucks made a couple of abortive attempts to invade again, but all were repulsed. It was a religious crusade.

We kept them supplied with a regular delivery of tea, coffee, soup, in giant thermos flasks. Annie cooked an endless assortment of pies, cakes and sausages. Press reporters came for interviews at odd times, and the TV cameras twice took videos of the encampment for the local news.

I occasionally chatted with some of the band as they sat around their stoves and campfires, in the field and by the roadside. They were mostly university students, off-duty workers, dropouts, with the odd seasoned campaigner scattered amongst them. Some only came for occasional shifts, some were there at regular times, some had apparently settled down to live there. They were always cheerful, motivated, inspired by their crusade, whatever they interpreted it to be. I had the impression that, for most of them, it gave an incentive to otherwise pedestrian lives.

Danny took to wandering down there regularly, and they welcomed him into their circle with affectionate greetings. Annie and

I often found him there, regaling a ring of intrigued faces with exotic stories and obscure general knowledge statistics. He blossomed under their tolerance like a professional entertainer.

Rain followed sun, followed by wind, followed by more rain, but the defenders stayed on undaunted. Even the sheep got used to them. It seemed that the situation was at a permanent stalemate.

Just as Annie and I were at a stalemate. We went about our lives like strangers in a foreign land. We ran the farm, the animals, the household as we had always done, but in a trance. My father and Jim drifted in and out but knew better than to intrude. We lived in a silent world, except for the distant background soundtrack from the throng by the lane. Even that became an irritant after a time. I wanted nothing to disrupt my torpor.

Then, almost a month after the opening skirmish, I received a call. I recognised the Lancashire accent. 'Oldfield? This is Jason Blackall. We'd like to come and see you.'

This was not something that aroused me. 'What about?'

'We want to discuss the situation.'

'Nothing to discuss.'

'Yes, there is. It can't go on forever like this.'

'It's out of my hands.'

'No, it's not. There's things you can do.'

All the old anxieties that I had repressed welled up again. 'What if I don't wish to do them?'

'You might if you hear what we have to say.'

What ruse had they dreamed up this time, I wondered. 'Say it on the phone.'

'We'd rather meet face to face.'

'I don't want to see your ugly face, and I'm sure you don't want to see mine.'

I could hear his sigh from eighty miles away. 'Look – we've got a proposition to put to you, and if you're any kind of businessman you'll at least want to hear it. You must want an end to this as much as we do.'

Well, he was right there at any rate. But the last thing I wanted was to have them sullying my home. 'Well, if you're really determined to come all this way, I'll meet you in our village. There's a pub there – the King's Head.'

'Good. We could see you there tomorrow evening.'

They were in a hurry. 'All right. Six o'clock. I'll be there.'

I didn't tell Annie where I was going – just said I was popping out for a bit and not to hold dinner. She didn't ask where. I got to the pub half an hour early, and sank a couple of stiff ones before they arrived. It was early and the place wasn't too full. It was one of those quintessential British drinking houses that had survived the onslaught of wine bars and modernised gastro-pubs, and still served real ale to the locals amongst old oak panels and spitting log fires. No piped music and Mexican tacos here. I chatted to Robbie the publican as I waited. He was as gnarled and twisted as a lightning-struck pine tree, but he'd been there forever, and I'd never known him take a day off from the business of wrecking the county's livers.

'How's yer battle goin' on up there?' he said. 'I hear you've got a reg'lar army defendin' the place.'

'Yes,' I said. 'I dunno what they're getting out of it, but they're a gang of hardened guerrilla fighters.'

'Good fer them. Least there's some people left who know what's right from wrong.'

'What does the village think, Robbie?' The rail route was a good mile away from where we were, but I was curious. 'Do they think we're doing the right thing keeping the trains at bay?'

'Bugger me, yes! No one hereabouts wants a bloody rail line runnin' through 'ere. Next thing we'll 'ave a motel on the village green and a McDonalds in the High Street.' He leaned confidentially across the mahogany bar top, impregnated with a century of beer spills. 'Are you goin' to win though, that's the thing? How long can you hold out agin' the buggers?'

'I don't know,' I muttered. 'However, the reason I'm here tonight is to meet some of the buggers. They're the owners of the Stainbridge quarry, which is the business at the heart of the whole thing.'

'The lot from Manchester?'

161

'Yes.'

'They comin' to twist yer arm?'

'Something like that. They're a tough lot, and they're desperate to sell.'

The light of battle glinted in his eye. 'Well, don't you let them threaten you. If it gets rough I'll throw them out on the street.'

I smiled. 'I don't think it'll get physical, Robbie. But just in case, keep your billiard cue handy.'

I took my glass to an alcove in the corner, nodding to old faces as I passed, and waited. The fire crackled, the regular customers gossiped, the beer kept flowing. I relaxed a little. I should do this more often, I thought.

They rolled up at five to six – Blackall senior and his sister, and to my surprise, Brad Faulkner. I hadn't anticipated that, but of course I should have guessed. His two sons were elsewhere, probably the grubbier pub down the street.

They looked around, saw me in my corner, bought some drinks, and came over. They were in shabby but formal suits, dressed to kill - the woman especially. I didn't get up. The three sat at the table – the Blackalls opposite on a big antique settle, Faulkner at the end, uncomfortable on a stool, since the only alternative was to sit next to me. We looked at each other. I waited for them to speak.

Blackall senior glanced around. 'Nice pub this.'

'Yes,' I said. 'We've got a few left.'

He sniffed. 'Wish we had. Ours are either shit-holes or poofs' cocktail bars.'

Silence again. He shifted on the settle cushion. 'So what are we goin' to do about this then?'

'You tell me. You wanted this meeting.'

He took a swig of his ale. 'That's nice.'

'Real Yorkshire ale,' I said.

He put the glass down. She hadn't touched hers yet. 'The thing is this, Oldfield. There's a helluva lot of money involved here. Money for us, money for Brad here, money for you. Now, I understand how you want to preserve your pretty farm, but surely there's a way we can do that and earn the money at the same time.'

'How?'

'Well...' he waved a vague hand, as if to conjure celestial solutions from the wood-smoked air.

His sister spoke. 'You can landscape rail lines. Banks, hedges, culverts.' Her lipstick almost illuminated our entire corner. 'You'd just have a slightly different outlook, that's all.'

'And what happens when they've put a main passenger line through?' I said. 'We'd have a very different outlook, and a very different noise level.'

She waved it away. 'That would take years.'

'Well, I intend to live for years.'

Brad Faulkner leaned forward. He hadn't said a word yet. 'They'll have to pay us even more compensation then.'

I stared back at him. 'Compensation, ah... there's a word.'

He banged his fist impotently on the table. 'What is it you want?'

'To be left alone, Brad.'

There was silence again. Blackall raised a finger with a dirty nail. 'The thing is this, Roger. Dragonsmead aren't going to give up on it. They'll demand the police do something about it, and the Royal Tank Regiment if necessary.'

'So? You said you had a proposition.'

'Not us, them. To make it easier, they've agreed to offer you their original deal. Even though, after the tribunal, they don't have to.'

I raised my eyebrows. 'They've told you that?'

'Yeh. Specifically.'

'They know about this meeting?'

'They know we're going to put the offer to you.'

That wasn't quite the same thing. 'Why would they do that? Stick to their offer?'

'Because they don't want this to drag on for months. They want to make it easier for everyone.'

'And richer for everyone.'

'Well, if you want to put it like that.' He sat back again, a mystified frown on his craggy face. 'I don't understand. What's wrong with being richer? How can you turn down a deal like this?'

I sighed. I was so weary of justifying myself. The logs on the fire next to us crackled, the room swayed with thick Yorkshire voices. 'It's just... just that I value some things more than money.'

His bottom lip jutted. He looked at his sister. She was staring at me as a cat stares at a big seagull - not sure whether it dared pounce or not. She had what looked like a gin and tonic in front of her, but she had only played with it.

'Well, the thing is this, Roger,' she said. 'We're going to get this through, whether you want it or not. The law says it must happen, and one way or another we're going to make it happen.'

I wondered whether she was the real brains of the business. I seagull-stared back at her. 'Well, go and tell that to the people stopping it happen. You're speaking to the wrong person.'

'Oh, come on,' she grunted. 'Don't tell us you're not behind all that.'

'No, I'm not. It all happened without my knowledge. I was as surprised as you.'

Brad spoke again. 'That's as mebbe. You could stop it if you wanted. You'd just have to say thank you all very much, and now bugger off.'

'Ah, Brad,' I said. 'Life's so simple for you, isn't it? Just say bugger off to anything you don't like, and all's right with the world.'

The look on his raddled face could have put the fire out.

Blackall was staring into his glass with a stony expression. Eventually he raised his head. 'This is getting us nowhere. Listen to me carefully, Oldfield. You either give in gracefully, and accept this very generous offer from the Collins's, or the gloves will come off.'

'Meaning?'

'Meaning it will get nasty. Very nasty. We've been patient so far, but you'll lose everything you care about. You'll wish to god you'd listened, taken the money, and settled for an easy life.'

I could feel my skin tightening. 'That sounds like a serious threat.'

'It is.' He glanced around. Robbie was watching us from behind the bar. Blackall drained his glass. 'We know how to deal with people like you.'

'You've already tried the scare tactics. You haven't succeeded so far.'

'We haven't started.' He heaved himself up from the settle. 'We can't do any more here, people. We've said all that needs to be said. We'll leave now.'

They departed. I looked at their glasses. Brad's was still half full, hers hadn't even a lipstick smear on it. The meeting had lasted barely ten minutes. A long way to come for that.

CHAPTER TWENTY SIX

munday. 16.32. sun and cold. 12C. went down to the camp agen tiday. i like going ther. they are nis peeple and they are not rood to me. they make tea for me and we al sit by the fir and tok and sing songs. i told them abowt al the difrent birds ther are on the farm wich they didn't no. and i told them about my insec colecshin wich im going to show them to morow. shepids pie agen for diner tonite. mum stil a bit sad

I know I was being stubborn. But when people threaten me I get bloody minded. Of course any sensible person would have taken the money and waved to all the people gazing out of the train windows as they whisked by. But I couldn't do it. Whatever the threats, I couldn't bring myself to throw in the towel and toss away all that we had fought for.

The thing is this. To outsiders it may have appeared that I was a reactionary. An old-fashioned codger who was locked into his narrow world, and just wanted to stop the march of progress. But it was more than that. I had seen some of the world. I hadn't always wanted to follow in my father's and grandfather's footsteps. As a teenager I had rebelled against the expected path, as teenagers do. I joined the army when I was eighteen, and went as a soldier to Afghanistan and Iraq.

There, I saw what mindless barbarism in other nations did to the lives of ordinary people. I saw the destruction of families, communities, whole cities by the forces of dictatorship, prejudice, religious extremism. I saw how ambition wrecked the lives of simple, hospitable, honest folk who only wished to get on with their lives, farming their land, rearing their children, loving the earth. I saw how the havoc wreaked on children's lives turned them into the next generation of angry killers. I saw the perverse side of human nature.

I left the army after four years, during which I witnessed things that no one should see. I realised that life at home wasn't so bad after all. It was Utopia compared to the life of others. And it needed to be protected. Things had happened during my absence – political controversy ravaging Westminster, foot and mouth disease ravaging farms, terrorist bombs ravaging London - and I felt that I needed to defend my small part of my homeland, just as I and my platoon had tried to defend the ruins of distant villages. We failed to preserve their heritage, but I needed to preserve mine. If only to preserve my sanity.

But of course I should have known that barbarism exists everywhere.

I didn't tell anyone about the meeting at the pub. Annie had taken to going to bed early as the nights drew in. She would read until I came up, and then put out the bedside light as soon as I got into bed. This time I put my own light on when she switched hers off. We lay there for some moments.

Eventually I said, 'Do you miss him?' It was the first time I had brought it up.

'No,' she said. She turned her head towards me. 'Of course I don't. It's just... I miss passion, people, bustle. I miss life.'

'Would you like to live in London on your own?'

'Don't be silly.'

'Well, you might have been tempted.'

'I might be tempted to go sailing round the world, but it's not realistic, is it?'

'Ah. Well, that's what he wants, so you could do it together.'

She raised herself onto her elbow and looked directly at me. Her finger stroked my shoulder. 'Anything I want to do together, I want to do with you.'

I stared at the ceiling. It needed painting. I turned over and switched off the light.

A few days later, I was doing something in one of the sheds when she came back from the lane with a box-full of empty mugs and plates. She looked worried.

'Have you seen Danny?' she said.

'Not since lunchtime. Then he wandered down to the camp.'

'He's not there. They said he stayed for half an hour or so, but then set off back here again. That was over an hour ago, and I haven't seen him since. He's nowhere in the house.'

I stopped what I was doing and we went to search. We called all around the farm buildings, we scoured the house again, we brought Jim and my father in on it. Danny was nowhere.

He had never gone AWOL before. I took the buggy and drove to the farthermost reaches of the land. I went into the woods, calling. We drag-netted the duck pond just in case, even though he knew not to go close to it. I checked our mobile phones, and his, which was sitting as usual unused in his room. There was nothing on any of them.

Then we rang the police.

This time Sergeant Jack was accompanied by a team of young policemen, headed by a brusque character who introduced himself as Inspector Alderson. They organised a search party to scour the surrounding countryside, and several of the protestors joined in. Lily too, when she got back from work. However, I knew there was not much point.

Two hours later, with dusk drawing in, the family sat with the two leading coppers in the kitchen. Annie was white-faced, shaking. I just felt numb.

'Can you think of any reason he may have disappeared?' asked the Inspector. 'Was he unhappy, or worried about anything?'

'He's been kidnapped,' I said.

A circle of faces stared at me with startled expressions. After a moment, he said, 'Why do you say that?'

'There are ruthless people who want to force my hand over the railway business. They've already threatened me. This is them.'

'That's a pretty serious accusation,' he said.

'They're pretty serious people.'

He looked at his sergeant. 'What was it that couple said to you down in the lane?'

Jack was gazing at me with a blank expression on his ruddy face. 'They thought they saw a car lower down after Danny left them. But it left. They presumed it had turned back because of the road blocks.'

'What kind of car?' I asked.

He shrugged. 'They didn't know. Just that it was black.'

'Why did nobody tell me this?'

'They didn't think it important. It was just a car.'

I said, 'We don't get just cars down here. That was probably it. Danny can't climb the wall. He has to walk several hundred yards along the lane to the farm entrance. Simple matter to waylay him.'

Annie gave a sob like a diver coming up for air. I put my hand on hers.

'Right,' said the senior man, getting up. 'We'll bring CID in on this. You'd better give me the names of all those involved with the rail thing. We'll get back and take a look at CCT cameras, although there aren't any until you get to the main roads. And you need to give me any photos of Danny that you have.'

Jack heaved himself up also. 'I'm so sorry, Roger. Let us know if you get anything.'

'Anything?'

'Demand. Communication. If you're right, you'll get a message. You'd better check your phone now.'

It had sat forgotten for the last hour in my pocket. I took it out and looked at it. An anonymous text said, 'SIGN OR PINE. NO COPS OR ITS CHOPS.' Just that.

'Christ!' I murmured. I only hesitated for a second, then handed it to the Inspector.

He looked at it. 'Poets, are they? Sent a while ago,' he said. 'We're too late to catch them. Come on, Jack. Back to the station.'

I put up my hand. 'It said, don't call the cops.'

'Don't worry,' he said. 'We had to know. These are amateurs. I doubt they'll harm him.' He held up an official finger. 'Don't communicate in any way with any of the parties involved with your dispute. We'll talk to them. And don't say anything to the press either. They'll be onto this soon.'

They went out, as Annie clung to me.

I was awake most of the night, thinking. Annie half snoozed beside me, tear stained, drugged with sleeping pills. I couldn't believe it was the Collins's. They'd never do anything so crude. Brad Faulkner would surely not risk anything so obviously incriminating. It had to be either his idiot sons or the Blackalls. My bet was on the latter. They had warned me. They were too astute to do it themselves. They must have used a third party.

We waited another terrible day. The farm was stuck in limbo. The trees barely waved, the air was paralysed, the river ran slower. The people at the camp gazed at us with blank faces when we visited. They did not know what to say.

I thought of going back to Manchester again with the shotgun. Bring Baghdad to England. But I knew that would probably make things worse.

Late that afternoon the landline rang. I answered. It was George Collins. We had not spoken since his visit to the farm. His deep voice was subdued.

'I've heard what has happened, Roger. I'm so sorry.'

'Have the police been to see you?'

'They were with us for an hour. I just want to assure you this wasn't us.'

'I didn't think so.'

'They didn't seem to have many ideas as to who is behind it. Have you?'

'Yes.'

'Not your boorish neighbour?'

'No.'

'No, probably not. My boorish vendors more likely.' I was silent. 'Have the national press been onto you yet?'

'No.'

'Well, they will. They've got hold of the story. They've been besieging our offices all afternoon. I'm afraid it's going to make headlines. But then that's no bad thing from your point of view.'

'Why?'

'It will deter anyone from doing anything too drastic.'

'Ah.'

There was an awkward pause. I had hardly spoken except in monsyllables. He said, 'Well, look - I've sent the Blackalls a message. I told them that the deal is off until your son is safely returned. It's the best I can do.'

'I see.'

'I, um... I hope that will produce the right response.' It was refreshing to have him on the defensive for once.

'Good. What then?'

'Then?'

'What happens about the railway?'

'Well, we'll just have to see. It's up to you.'

I rang off. I was too dead to speak further.

In Iraq, two of our platoon were captured by the Taliban. We found their mutilated corpses a week later. I know it wasn't the same, but I could not get those images out of my mind.

CHAPTER TWENTY SEVEN

No entry

The press were onto us that evening, half the night, and first thing next day. First the locals, then the nationals. The phone rang incessantly. Why did it always seem shriller when it was the media? Either I or Annie answered, and all we said was, yes, Danny had gone missing, and yes, the police were looking for him, and yes, that was all we could tell them.

The headlines were already up, with bright pictures of Danny's happiest face, lifted presumably from the television footage.

DISABLED SON KIDNAPPED IN RAIL DISPUTE.

AUTISTIC DANNY CAUGHT IN RAILWAY WAR.

The TV stations of course wanted to come again, but we cut them off sharply. They had plenty of material from before anyway, so they contented themselves with showing extracts on the news. I wondered whether Danny was able to watch.

Lily had ridden off on Shard early. Scouring the land, looking for clues perhaps. Something to keep occupied. My father prowled around like a lost badger.

'I hope all this isn't going to scare them into doing anything stupid,' I said to Annie and him in the kitchen. The papers were spread out in front of us.

'Nah,' my father answered. He was looking as gaunt as we were. He had lost his Monopoly partner. 'They'll know the whole country will be wanting their heads if they harm him. Innards too. They've lost all sympathy.' It was a nice try, but I wasn't convinced.

I still had to do the farm rounds. I did everything automatically, without thinking. Annie followed me round. She couldn't bear to be on her own. She touched me and held on at every available opportunity. I didn't mind. I was beyond reacting.

Someone from the CID rang and asked all the same questions the police inspector had asked. I gave the same answers. They said that they were working on the case, and somebody would come and talk to us, but they never did.

For want of anything better, I decided to do some detective work myself.

There were two places the suspect car would have had to pass, if indeed it was the vehicle involved. One was Jim and Doris's cottage, which was down by the lane, and the other was Mike Foster's farm two miles on. In between the two lay fields, and woodland, and open heath, and very little else. That evening, when all the farm work was done, and Annie was apathetically preparing to cook something for dinner in the kitchen, I wandered down the drive to the cottage.

It was a small whitewashed place, that had squatted behind its narrow patch of garden by the roadside for two centuries or more. Grass fringed its pathways. Vegetables, tomatoes, and raspberries grew in their seasons in a bed alongside, and summer flowers framed the tiny lawn, lovingly tended by Doris. Generations of farm workers had occupied it, and over the years various modifications had improved it, but it still remained in essence a humble dwelling that might have graced the pages of Thomas Hardy or D.H. Lawrence.

As I approached the oak front door under its minimal porch, I could dimly hear a television commentary filtering from inside. I knew the pair would be watching, seated in their separate floral covered armchairs, drinks in hand - Yorkshire ale for Jim, tonic with a splash of gin for Doris. I did not often visit unannounced, but I was always welcome. I knocked, lifted the ancient latch, and opened the door a foot. 'Anyone at home?' I called. 'Mind if I come in?'

A little gasp from Doris, and a flurry of activity. 'Oh! Come in, come in, Mr Oldfield' she cried, and hissed some urgent instructions at her husband.

I ducked under the doorway, entered the living room, and went back half a century in time. Logs burned in the iron fireplace, lamps glowed inadequately from under parchment shades, a worn Axminster carpet covered most of the stone floor. The old couple were hastily piling newspapers and debris to the side, and dusting off the small sofa underneath the curtained window. 'Don't mind the mess,' said Doris, bobbed grey hair flopping around her pixie face. 'We was just wotchin' the news, though God knows why. It's mis'rable as ever.'

Jim was switching off the TV. It was one of those old-fashioned box sets, that might have fetched good money in an antique shop. I'd often offered to get them a modern one, but they always insisted they were happy with it. They would switch between the BBC channels and little else. Netflix and Prime were foreign words to them.

'Sorry to interrupt you,' I said. 'I just wanted a quick word about the situation.'

Doris gave a great sigh as she gestured for me to sit on the sofa. Jim was pouring me a glass without asking. Cooking smells drifted from the back kitchen. 'Terrible, terrible, Roger!' she said, wide mouse's eyes immediately moist in her diminutive face. She had after all been almost a second mother for most of Danny's life. 'That poor lad - who could do such a thing? We bin awake half the nights thinkin' about it, haven't we, Jim.'

He nodded, handing me the glass of brown ale. 'Buggers! I'd skin 'em alive.'

She poked the fire into a blaze. 'I just hope they're treatin' him right. How he's copin' with strange people, lord knows.'

'Well, you know Danny,' I said, in a poor attempt at reassurance. 'He's probably boring them to death with weather statistics.'

Doris chuckled, nodding in agreement. The pair sat back in their chairs. 'What are the police sayin'?'

'Not much. They're working on it, but they don't tell us anything.' I leaned forward. 'That's why I wanted to talk to you, Doris. You see most of what's happening out there in the lane.' I knew she always took note of anything passing by, so rare were the occasions on our remote country road. The arrival of the protest army had been a source of endless entertainment for her. 'I was just wondering... you know that a car was reported being seen there, about the time Danny disappeared?'

She nodded. 'Oh, yes. A black one. I'd wondered whose it was.'

I blinked. 'You saw it?'

174

'Yes. I told the coppers.' She gestured towards the window. 'It passed by 'ere. Then I suppose it saw all the hullabaloo goin' on down there at the camp, and it turned about and came back again a bit later. Goin' quicker that time.'

'Could you see who was in it?'

She shook her head, wiping her eyes with a small patterned handkerchief. 'I only got a glimpse as it passed the garden wall. It were black, I know that. Or mebbe dark blue.'

'I don't suppose you had any idea of the make?'

Another shake. 'Didn't look that new. One o' they Japanese jobs most like.'

'A Toyota or a Honda, you mean?'

Jim spoke up for the first time. 'It were summat like that. Doris dunno the makes. Ours is a Mazda, and she thought it were similar.' He wrinkled his weather tortured nose. 'They all look alike, the Jap ones.'

The pair had a fifteen year-old car which, with shopping trips and the occasional Sunday outing, did about as much mileage a year as did one of my sheep.

'That's interesting, Doris,' I said. 'How much time was there between its passing?'

She pondered, her small spider's fingers scratching at her fringe. 'Dunno. A while. Mebbe fifteen, twenty minutes. I wondered what they'd bin doin', but I thought they'd probably bin watchin' the fun and games at the camp.' Her eyes welled up again. 'If I'd known Danny was there, I'd have... I'd have...' She tailed off and blew her nose. What she might have done nobody knew.

I sat back. There wasn't much else she could tell me. It was just a smidgin, but it confirmed the theory. We talked a bit more about nothing in particular, and then I finished my beer and got up.

'Well, I won't keep you from your supper, people. Thank you. I just wanted to confirm what we were thinking.'

Doris opened the door for me. A blast of chilly night air knifed in. 'I do hope the poor lad gets home quick, Roger. We're prayin' for him every night.'

I kissed her damp cheek, and thanked her, although I didn't set much store by prayers. The nations that prayed the most, did the most damage in my experience.

'See you in the morning, Jim,' I called over her shoulder. And I returned to my own silent dinner table.

Next morning I left everything to Jim, and took the Jeep to Mike Foster's farm. I timed it to catch him in the parlour at milking time, which was a pretty safe gamble. Mike farmed more cows than I did, and less sheep. He didn't have as many high pastures as I did, but his Shorthorn herd was top grade.

I drove up his drive between white fencing - smarter than ours - to the farm buildings. Sure enough, he was there in the long modern milking shed, alongside Charlie Porter his cow man, checking the milk pipes. Snorting and stamping and the rythmic pumping of the milking machines filled the air, and the smell of straw and cows was no different to mine.

We greeted each other with few preliminaries, as farmers do when on the job.

'Any news?' Mike asked, wiping his hands on his work overalls.

I shook my head. 'We're just waiting, waiting. It's all we can do. But meanwhile I'm trying to find out what little I can.' I leaned on the rail beside one of the handsome looking cows, who gave me the briefest of glances before returning her attention to the feeding trough. 'You know that a car was seen in the lane at about the time Danny vanished?'

Mike nodded, his round face the picture of sympathy. He had three children himself, still at school age. I didn't need to tell him how I was feeling. 'I heard that,' he said. 'Any idea whose it was?'

'No. There's very little we know about it. But that's why I'm here. I just wondered whether you or the missus, or any of your men might have seen it.'

He turned immediately, and called to Charlie Porter who was down the other end of the cow line. 'Charlie! Come here a moment.' He turned back. 'Charlie thought he saw something. He told the police about it.'

Charlie came up. Big young man, weighing almost as much as one of their cows, but with a more expressive face.

'Tell Roger about the car you saw, Charlie,' said his employer.

Charlie scratched his beard. It compensated for his prematurely receding hairline. 'Well, it weren't much of a look. I were down in the bottom field by the lane, when it passed by. I only saw the top half across the wall. There were a couple of people in it - both men by the look.'

'Both men?'

'Think so. It went towards your circus down there, and I didn't think much about it. But then twenty minutes later, I was back in the yard, and I heard it comin' back t'other way. Goin' quite fast. Caught a glimpse, but couldn't see who was in it this time. I told the police that.'

'Was it black?' I said. 'Japanese?'

'Could have bin. Dark colour anyway. Don't often get stray cars like that along this way.'

That was all either of them could tell me. I said thank you, and went home. Doubtless Sherlock Holmes or Hercule Poirot would have deduced much more from such evidence, but there was little more I could do on the detective level.

Annie didn't ask where I'd been. She had given up asking any sort of questions.

CHAPTER TWENTY EIGHT

No entry

Two days passed. Days that crawled by in a fog, yet days that we would never forget. Somehow we ate and slept. Somehow the farm kept going. Somehow we kept breathing. It's not until you lose a child that you know the elemental agony of it.

As we lay in bed on the second night, Annie said, 'We should do it. We should give them what they want. Nothing is worth this.'

I lay silent for a long moment. Part of me agreed. The bloody-minded part said, why should we surrender to such perversity? Why should we let the bad guys win? It was that instinct that had kept me fighting the futile wars in the desert.

But then Danny was worth a hundred bad guys.

'Let's talk about it tomorrow,' I said.

Tomorrow came, after another sleepless night. Dawn had not long broken, the land lay under a layer of malicious cloud. The air sagged with the misery. Every activity took place in slow, agonised motion.

We sat around the kitchen table - myself and Annie and Lily and my father. The room had not yet warmed up, and we all had sweaters on, and hands round mugs of tea. I checked my phone for messages every few minutes, but it remained as vacant as my diary.

'We'll take a vote on it,' I said. 'Do we agree to the railway, provided Danny is returned safe and sound? All in favour?'

It only took a minute or two, then the hands went up one by one. Mine was the last.

'Bastards,' muttered my father. 'They'll find them eventually. Then we'll send in a lynch mob.'

'You'll have to tell the police,' said Annie.

'I don't know how such things are organised,' I said. 'I'll talk to the lawyer.'

'Is that necessary?' Her eyes were dim with too much weeping. 'Won't that hold things up?'

178

'It's not a simple business,' I said. 'They'll want proof of the deal, and we'll want proof of Danny's safety.'

As soon as Driscoll's London office opened, I rang. His secretary put me through.

'Hello, Mr Driscoll,' I said. 'Do you know our situation?'

'Yes, Roger.' He used his personal voice. 'I read the papers. I'm so sorry. Do you know who's behind it?'

'We have our suspicions, but we can't prove anything. There are various parties who might have a hand in it. Meanwhile we need to get our son back as soon as possible, for his sake. We want to conclude the deal with Dragonsmead. We want to end this saga.'

I could almost hear his brain ticking at the other end. 'Do the police know of your decision?'

'Not yet. And the decision is ours in any case.'

'Very well,' he said eventually. 'The kidnappers will want proof. I imagine they're a criminal outfit employed by whoever instigated it. We'll have to agree a contract with the Collins's which they see as watertight, but conditional upon Danny's safe return. Will the Collins family agree to that?'

'I think so.'

'How are the kidnappers communicating with you?'

'They aren't yet. Except for one text message. Untraceable.'

'Right. Well, no doubt they will. I'll get onto it. Meanwhile talk to the police.'

I did. I got through to someone called Detective Inspector Stephens at Barnard Castle CID, who was apparently in charge of our case.

'I thought you were going to come and speak to us,' I said without preliminaries. I was in no mood to be diplomatic.

'We were,' he replied. 'But we're very preoccupied following up on all the parties involved with your case.' It was another disembodied voice whose owner I could not picture. 'It's quite a complex situation you have there.' There was irony in the tone.

'You could say that. However we want to simplify it. We want to give the kidnappers what they want.'

'You mean the deal on your land?'

'Yes.'

There was a pause. 'I'm not sure that's wise, Mr Oldfield. I'm sure we'll find these people.'

'You may, but it might be too late for Danny. Have you talked to the Blackall quarry mob?'

'We've talked to everyone. We're still talking. But of course they all deny knowledge at the moment.'

'Well, this is all about a stupid railway. That isn't as important as our son's life. So we want to give them what they're demanding. If you can catch them after, well and good.'

His voice was non-committal. Whether he agreed, or whether he was disappointed at having to surrender to the enemy, I couldn't tell. 'Very well,' he said. 'Do what you have to do. Meanwhile we'll continue our investigations.'

Continue investigations. How often does one hear that on the news, and how little does it mean? But I felt a small lifting of the pressure on my mind with the prospect of action.

Another day passed in a somnolent daze. Wheels were presumably turning elsewhere, but there was no indication at the farm. All our systems were in semi-paralysis. I knew I had to keep going for the sake of everyone, but the agony of waiting was almost unendurable.

The gods, however, work in strange ways.

At around six o'clock that evening, when dusk had fallen, the landline phone rang. I went to take it in the hall, my heart pounding. This was not an insistent press ring - I knew there was a difference. But neither was it anything else expected.

'Detective Inspector Stephens here, Mr Oldfield. We've got your son.'

I collapsed to a sitting position on the stone flags of the hallway. I could not speak.

'Are you there?'

'Yes,' I whispered. Annie had come out, and was staring wide-eyed. 'What...? How...? Is he all right?'

'Yes, he's fine. Quite cheerful actually. Seemed to think it was an adventure.'

'What happened?'

'That's what we're trying to find out. He was dumped in the dark this evening somewhere close to the station, and told to come in. There's no question he was taken. We need to talk to him for an hour or so. See if there's anything he can tell us. Then, if you like, we'll send him home in a police car.'

'No, no. We'll come to you. We'll come and get him.'

'Very well. I just wanted to let you know as soon as possible. He seems to be fine.'

I had never driven to the town so fast. 'Don't kill us on the way,' said Annie, hanging on.

We reached the police station, and were shown into a back interview room. There sat Danny, still in the same clothes, a large polystyrene cup and a larger muffin in front of him. He was swinging his legs on a chair as he spoke, mouth full, to the DI across the table. A younger detective sat next to his boss, and a police-woman in uniform stood at the side. When Danny saw us, he grinned, and then endured our suffocating hugs with patient endurance.

'Are you all right, darling?' asked Annie eventually, tears flowing unashamedly as she smoothed his tangled hair.

He pushed her hand from his head. 'Yeh, they've given me apple juice and chocolate muffin, my fav'rite.'

'Yes, but before that, when you were sleeping somewhere. Did they hurt you?'

He shook his head. 'They were all right. Not very nice food, but they let me watch telly, and the lady played cards with me. I won.'

We looked up at the detective. Now I could put a face to him. He was a thin man with a hook nose and a world-weary expression which said, I've seen everything now. 'It seems he was taken by two men,' he said, 'and driven with a hood over his head for what seems to be an hour or so, and then kept in a windowless room or cellar, where a woman saw to most of his needs. However he seems to remember quite a lot about the journey. He's telling us about that now. So if you don't mind, I'd like him to carry on with the story.'

181

We nodded and sat to one side, agog.

He turned back to Danny. Spoke to him as if commiserating with an old friend whose wife had inexplicably walked out on him. 'So, Danny, you were telling me that you recognised the bends and the bridges all the way towards Barnard Castle here, and then you think you crossed the river on the big bridge. Is that right?'

Danny nodded, still chewing. 'I heard the water.'

'But you couldn't see anything at all?'

Shake of the head.

'Were you lying down, or sitting up?'

'Sitting up. But I couldn't see.'

'Was it a big car?'

'It was a Honda Civic one point six litre diesel.'

The room froze. The DI shook his head as if to loosen his brain. 'How do you know that, Danny?'

'I could hear the engine. It was the same as Joe my taxi man drives. I asked the man how big the engine was. He told me one point six, so I knew it had to be a Honda.'

The man glanced at his junior with eyebrows high. 'Better check that.' The other nodded, looking equally bemused.

'What do you remember then?' said the DI.

Danny pulled his sour face. 'We went a long way on another road. I didn't like it with the hood on.'

'Were you frightened?'

Nod. 'But they were quite nice after.'

'Can you remember anything about the road?'

'We went through people working on the road, and we had to stop for the bulldozer.'

'Bulldozer?'

'It sounded like a bulldozer, and one of the men said a rude word. Then we went on again, and we passed through three villages.'

'How did you know?'

'We had to go slow, and there were more cars and stuff.'

The DI glanced at his junior. 'Has to be the Darlington Road. There are road works there, working at night. And those are the villages along the route.' He turned back. 'That's clever of you, Danny. Then what do you remember?'

'We went through a big town with lots more cars and buses, and then we stopped at the fact'ry where we stayed.'

'Factory?'

'There were big gates the man had to open. And he said, park behind the truck.'

'Remember anything else?'

'It smelt dusty and it was beside a railway.'

The DI's eyebrows went higher still. 'How do you know that?'

'I heard the trains when I was in the room and they took the hood off.'

He glanced at us. 'It's Darlington all right.'

Ironic how Darlington and railways seemed to feature so much in our story. We were as riveted as were the police.

Danny went on, enjoying the audience. 'They gave me a marg'rita pizza for supper, but it wan't my fav'rite. My fav'rite is pepperoni. Then we watched some telly, but not my fav'rites. Then they put me to bed on a smelly couch, and shut the door. It was dark, and I was a bit frightened, so I counted the trains. There were trains at seventeen minutes past seven, and twenty-six minutes past seven, and...'

'Jesus!' exclaimed the DI to his junior. 'Take this down!' The young man started scribbling.

'...forty-one past seven, and forty-nine past seven, and twelve past eight, and then I fell asleep.' He took another swig at his drink. 'Then in the morning before breakfast, there were trains at twenty-two past six, and thirty-five past six, and...' The list went on.

The DI sat back in his chair, and stared at Danny as if he was the Angel Gabriel. 'Mother of God!' he exclaimed. 'If all our witnesses were like this, we'd have eliminated crime from the earth long ago.'

His companion stopped writing, and gazed at the list. 'We can almost pinpoint the exact spot with these, sir.'

'We bloody sure can. Get onto it now. Get the timetables.'

The young man rose, and scuttled from the room. The rest of us took a collective breath. The espionage thriller continued.

'Last thing, Danny. Do you think you would recognise the three people who were with you, if you saw them again?'

He nodded. 'The lady was quite nice, but not very pretty.'

'And the men?'

'One was old with an ugly beard, and the other had tattoos on his arms. They weren't nasty, but they were rude about me.'

'Rude?'

'They said I was a dickhead who didn't know my rude word from my elbow.'

The cop chuckled. To us he said, 'You've brought him up well.' Then back to Danny. 'Well, you've proved it was them who are the dickheads, eh?'

'Yeh. Are there any more muffins?'

Annie clasped my arm as she wiped her tears with a hanky. 'I think he'll want that on his gravestone. Are there any more muffins?'

CHAPTER TWENTY NINE

thirsday. 7.12. Rain. 13C. cows under the trees. rooks here now. robins and chafinch in the gardin. i was taken away by peeple and hiden in a factry. they gave me piza and we wochd telly and played cards and i went to bed there. then they took me to the polis station and i told the polis evry thing. it was ecsiting. its nice to be home agen. mumdad happy. they sed they wer fritind abowt me but they didn need to be. wen i tok to peepl they stop being rood to me

It didn't take the police long. They can shift themselves quite quickly when they have a case that interests them. They pinpointed the place very easily, and raided it that same night. Whether just a few plain clothes officers, or a full firearms team with automatics, stun grenades and tear gas, they didn't say. It turned out to be a builders yard, stretching beside the mainline railway on the outskirts of the town. Another ramshackle family outfit whose Dickensian files showed accounts with various providers for materials - bricks, cement, gravel, stone. One of their largest suppliers was Blackall Quarries.

'Bloody fools!' said the DI when he turned up at the farm next day. He came in a smart anonymous car, accompanied by the same junior companion. He marched into the house with scarcely a glance at his surroundings. 'How they thought they'd get away with such a crude stunt, God knows. Anyway, we've arrested the three owners - husband, wife, and son. Of course they drive a black Honda Civic, and they all fit Danny's descriptions. But I need him to identify the photos. Once he's done that we'll tackle the Blackall lot. That will be a bit more difficult - establishing the link and the instructions and so on, but we'll get them. They must have made some sort of deal.'

'Why do you think they let him go?' Annie asked in her risen-from-the-dead voice.

He threw her a lugubrious look. 'Either they chickened out because of all the publicity, or they were told to give him back because the quarry deal was off.' His voice grumbled with long-held contempt for all the imbeciles in the world. 'Amateurs!'

I wondered whether he'd call them that if he hadn't had my son's evidence, but I didn't say so.

It only took Danny seconds to identify the photos. Then he lost interest and went back to updating his diary, weather records, and collection statistics. It had just been another nameless event in the uncoiling of the earth's orbit as far as he was concerned.

Everything changed after that. The newspapers reported Danny's reappearance with loud fanfares, followed by lurid accounts of the raid on the kidnappers' yard, and even more exaggerated conjectures about the involvement of the Blackalls. Then, with no more to go on, they lost interest and returned to less important matters such as global warming and the collapse of the economy. The lawyer abandoned the idea of resurrecting the deal with the Collins family. Our own family got back to the business of running the farm, the protestors continued their vigil by the lane, and the weather got colder and wilder as winter approached. But we all knew that the character of the situation was no longer the same.

A fortnight after Danny's return - a fortnight during which the whole issue of the railway had started to fade to the back of my mind, like a nightmare that one knew one had dreamt, but couldn't quite remember - I received another call from George Collins. He didn't even bother to introduce himself, since he was used to people recognising his voice.

'Roger, I'm delighted everything has worked out well for you. You must be so relieved to have your son back.'

'Yes,' I said, waiting for the real reason for his call.

'I need to see you again. I'm planning to take a break at the Litton Manor Hotel next week. It's about twenty miles from you. They have

186

a good restaurant, and I'd like to invite you and your wife to dinner with me. Would you come? I'd send my car to pick you up, so you wouldn't have to drive.'

'What for, George?' It was the first time I'd used his christian name, but things were different now.

'I have a proposition to put to you.'

The dream reared up like a mushroom cloud again. 'Haven't we run out of propositions?'

'No. This is different. I think you'd be interested. If not, well, we'll just have a nice dinner, and talk about other things.'

I hesitated. 'Will Martin be with you?'

'No. He's left the company.'

'Oh?'

'He and Julia have split up. Good thing really. She was always too tough for him.'

Would Annie have been too tough for him, I wondered? He went on. 'He's gone off to follow his dream, scouring the oceans to discover when the human race will be obliterated.'

'Ah. Might that happen before we have dinner?'

He chuckled. 'It might do. But if not, we can at least go out with a final fling. Please say yes.'

I did. It was against my instincts, but I had abandoned all attempts to follow my instincts.

Litton Manor was one those converted manor house hotels that Britain has so wantonly scattered around its landscapes. Stone built, excessively spacious, languidly stylish, surrounded by gardens developed by generations of green-fingered stewards, they are the quintessential domains of the upper classes transformed into luxury retreats for the nouveaux riche.

We had been there a couple of times, but only for the most special of occasions. This was an occasion of a different hue, and Annie was hesitant about it considering her liaison with Collins junior, but I persuaded her. I thought it was a chance to show her what a dreadful alternative fate she had escaped. I had ceased to conjecture about the reason for the meeting. I was immune to the twists the story might take.

We decided we should go in fully armed, so we both dressed up. She looked superb in a Marks and Spencer job, copied from some Paris fashion house. I brought my tie.

Harry, the chauffeur, deposited us at the front door, having chatted en route about the weather and the football and the price of beer, but telling us little about what we were there for. He then drove off again to one of those mystery diversions that retainers find to pass the time in between duties.

Annie gazed up at the ancient facade of the house, dozing like a sleepy giant in the last rays of sunlight, and sighed. 'Well, perhaps it's all worth it if it gives us this sort of break once in a while.'

We entered, and the Meissen-china receptionist took our coats, and directed us straight to the dining room. 'Mr Collins is expecting you,' she said unnecessarily. 'Welcome to Litton Manor.'

They were already drawing the curtains and lighting candles on the dining tables. Ancestral owners and shining stallions gazed at us with oil-painted hauteur from the walls, silver and cut-glass flashed as we passed, the smells of old stone and timber mingled with those of haute cuisine.

It was relatively early, and there were only a few tables occupied. George Collins was seated at the most secluded one, tucked into the wide bay-window alcove. With him was a slender woman in a floating silken dress that had probably cost the price of six breeding cows. George rose as we approached. Annie received the full broadside of the Collins smile as he shook hands.

'Delighted to see you again,' he said. 'It's been too long. And hopefully under happier circumstances this time.'

'Yes,' she replied, in a slightly strained voice. I knew she was thinking of her dalliance with his son.

'And this is my wife, Claudia.' He introduced the woman with a wave of the hand.

She smiled. 'Hello.' She had Martin's blue eyes, and tight-cut, untinted dark hair. I guessed she was probably ten years younger than her husband. I was vaguely surprised to find her there. It hadn't occurred to me to conjecture about his domestic life, but of course he had one.

He indicated the two chairs opposite, and said, 'A glass of champagne to start? That's what we're having.'

We didn't refuse. The head waiter had magically appeared almost before we were seated, and Collins waved at their flutes. 'The same for our guests, Dickie. And some of those terrific stuffed olives you do.'

'Certainly, Mr Collins.' And away he went, under full sail.

I was puzzled. 'They know you here?'

He showed no expression. 'They should do. I own the place.'

We both sat back with startled looks. He chuckled then. 'The company has a number of select hotels around the country. But this one is especially valued. Tell them about our colourful past, Claudia.'

She was sipping her champagne with elegant delicacy. She put the glass down, and glanced about the room. 'I grew up here. It was my family home.' She had that same accentless upper class voice that managed to be both amiable and aloof at the same time. 'We were forced to sell it about twenty years ago. My father couldn't afford to keep it up, having made some bad business decisions. George came to view it, and saw its potential for a country house hotel.' Her eyelids drooped as she threw him a glance. 'He also saw the potential in me. I was only twenty-four at the time, and still living at home. He was considerably older than me, but that didn't stop him from pulling out all the stops to woo me. My parents were very against the match, assuming he was just wanting another scalp to his belt, but he persisted, and as you know, there's nothing like diligent attention from a glamorous older man to break down a girl's resistance.'

'Yes, I know a bit about that,' said Annie, throwing me a cheeky glance.

'Hey! I'm not that much older,' I said.

George had been listening to his wife with amused tolerance. There was obviously a mutually respectful relationship between the pair. 'If you'd seen her at twenty-four, you'd have known why I was so besotted,' he said.

'Ah well, I know a bit about *that*,' I said, returning Annie's look.

His wife ignored his compliment and went on. 'Anyway, it rapidly became clear that I was part of the deal to buy the house. My father blatantly used me as a bargaining point to secure as good a price as he could from George's company, and I was handed over like a dancing girl to a sheik's harem.'

George chuckled. 'Bloody cheap at the price too.'

I was starting to like him better. There was another side to him than the copybook tycoon. But then there are other sides to everyone.

'I rather like that story,' said Annie.

'Well, yes, it makes a good fairy tale,' said Claudia, toying with the stem of her glass. 'However, these things are never plain sailing, are they?'

'Careful now,' warned her husband with a glint.

'I soon found out that being married to a sheik is not all hearts and flowers and Arabian perfume. Ambitious men can be very demanding.' She gave him a tolerant smile. 'However, over time I found out how to tame him.'

He shrugged like an obedient mastiff. 'Yes, she has me completely under her thumb now.'

A wealth of family history lurked in that brief exchange. I had often noted how fierce corporate warlords in their offices could become puppy dogs at home. Women are the real strongmen in this world. They just don't use money and guns to prove it.

Annie spoke to his wife in that intimate way they use when identifying with other women. 'So do you miss the family home?'

Claudia gazed distantly at the far wall with its family paintings. 'It's strange, seeing it in this quite different guise. But then buildings need to be transformed every so often, don't they, if they are to survive.' Her diamond earrings glinted in sympathy with her nostalgia. 'I can't say I'm thrilled at its transformation, but I'm glad other people are enjoying it now.'

I was still vaguely puzzled at the situation. 'So, do you visit often?'

She deferred to her husband. His polished magnate's skin glowed in the candlelight, but he looked marginally awkward. 'Occasionally. We like to make a sentimental return now and again. We do love this part of the world.'

Annie said, 'So you were familiar with these parts long before the Blackall quarry project?'

'Oh, yes.' He was dismissive. 'In fact it was how I came to know about their situation.'

'So...' I didn't know how to frame the question. 'So, if you and your wife are both so familiar with the Dales... you must understand our feelings about the railway.'

There was a silence. She gazed at him, as if to say, this is your baby, chum, don't look to me for help.

'Of course I do,' he said eventually, playing with a knife on the thick white table cloth. 'Don't think I haven't felt some ambivalence over the whole thing.'

'I would never have known it,' I said bluntly.

He had the grace to show a flicker of remorse. 'You can never admit ambivalence when doing business, Roger. Probably not when breeding sheep either.' He had me there. 'But when something as big as this comes along, I'm afraid business instincts outweigh poetic ones.' He took a deep breath. 'However, that's what I wanted to talk to you about...'

We had to wait in suspense. The waiter returned with our champagne and a bowl of olives. He had menus under his arm, which he distributed. 'The fish of the day is fresh river trout, Mr Collins,' he said. 'And the chef's special is venison bourguignon.'

'Thank you, Dickie,' replied the host. 'Give us a couple of minutes, and we'll order.'

The man departed after the obligatory unfurling of napkins on laps, a ritual I never quite understood.

'Let's choose dinner,' said George. 'Then we'll get to the less serious matters.'

We studied the menus. The dishes were all described in exotic French terms which only a native of France would understand, and not many of them. For simplicity's sake I chose two items which I did recognise - *coquilles St Jacques*, and *filet de boeuf au poivre,* the latter described as 'locally sourced', though knowing my beef as I did I had my doubts as to how far 'locally' extended. Annie threw me an amused look, and said she'd have the same. She knew she'd have to cut my steak up for me, but she was used to that.

When we had all perused enough, George put down his menu, took another mouthful of champagne, and said, 'So, people, this is the situation. Confidentially, the police can probably prove the Blackall family's idiotic conspiracy to have your son kidnapped. It was a last desperate ploy on their part. The company is about to go into receivership. However this will only hasten the process. They are in deep trouble, and may well end up in prison.' He had the expression of a man torn between regret and triumph. 'We have done a deal to take the whole miserable outfit off the Receiver's hands for considerably less than we were originally going to pay. He's only too glad to be rid of the mess. We are going to go ahead with the deal, whatever comes of the rail situation.'

He stopped then, and fixed us both with his businessman's stare, ambivalence forgotten. 'But we still of course want to access all that magnificent stone. So here's my proposal. We forget about the rail idea, and go for something completely different.'

'What?' I said.

'A canal.'

Pause. 'Canal?'

He held the suspense like a magician about to produce a ten-pound note from thin air. 'Canals are being restored and extended all over the country. I've had my people look into it thoroughly. We can build a narrow canal from the quarry, along roughly the same line as the railway was going to take. It need be less than ten miles long. Once it's past Faulkner's and your properties, we can then transfer everything onto a rail line alongside the roads to the Darlington network. It will mean marginally higher transport costs, but the beauty is that we can sink it below ground level across your property, so you wouldn't see it except from above. We would only need a single lock to lower the level enough, and we'd place that on

Faulkner's land. He's in no position to protest.'

He paused, watching our bemused faces. Then he went on. 'The advantages to you would be an invisible and virtually silent method of transport, much simpler bridges to cross from one side to the other, and, best of all, this would preclude any chance of the route being developed into a mainstream passenger line.' He sank into a minor key for the final flourish. 'And we'd offer you the same deal as before.'

He waited, studying us for our reactions. He got none. We were too stunned.

The waiter returned to take our order, and Collins gave it to him with brusque dispatch, before returning his focus to us. He lowered his voice, and glanced around to confirm that no one else was in earshot. 'There is another factor, which you might want to consider. Canal boating holidays are becoming hugely popular these days. Narrow-boat hire is big business. We could go into partnership on a boat yard built close to the quarry, and allow boating along the length of the canal, to time with the couple of days a week we'd be transporting the limestone. The profits would be considerable, and you'd be encouraging an environmentally friendly leisure activity.'

He sat back, professional presentation completed.

I was thinking of Danny's comment all those weeks ago in the lamb shed. 'They should build a canal. That's how they used to do it once.' Out of the mouths of babes...

'Was this your idea?' I asked.

'Well, actually,' he said, picking up his glass, 'my son Martin first suggested it. Just as a hypothetical possibility. At first I dismissed it, but when we looked into it the feasibility became more apparent.'

Annie said, 'And our son Danny suggested it to him.'

His eyes widened. 'Really?' She nodded. 'Well, perhaps we should have Danny on the board of directors.'

She smiled. 'You could do worse.'

'How would you finance it?' I asked.

'The same way we'd finance the railway. Bank loans. Paid off as we went along. We'd save a lot of the construction costs by using our own stone from the quarry - the inferior stuff that isn't good enough for buildings. The banks will be much happier with something like this, than with the ongoing controversy over the railway.'

His wife was watching us with detached amusement. She was used to her husband's grandiose stratagems. She probably considered them in the same light as her children's brick castles in the nursery.

I looked at Annie. She looked at me. Her eyes were shining. I knew the game was up, even before I'd had a chance to consider the implications.

I'm sure the dinner was excellent, but I hardly tasted any of it.

CHAPTER THIRTY

satiday. 7.16. stratus clouds. 10C. cold stay in bed. mum say she bring me brekfist in bed speshil treat. poridge and huny my no 2 favrit. mumdad went owt to diner yestiday and we are goin to bild a canal. i can wotch the boats bringing the stones. its ecsiting. damis the deer was on the hil agen this morning. his wife was ther too and a baby deer. i wish i wos a deer. or perhaps a giraf. i have 237 things in my colecshin now and 22 insecs in my insec jar. only 4 have died. i qwite like winter

It took three years. Three years while the seasons came and went, the river ebbed and flowed, the beasts bred and died, the birds flew off and returned. Three years whilst vast machines gouged the earth across the valley, and fleets of trucks ploughed up the tracks and the lanes, and the clanking and clatter became an intermittent part of our day-to-day mood music. Three years whilst Lily became chief stable mistress at her stud, and Danny extended his volumes of records and calculations, and my father drank his arthritis under the table, and Annie and I became friends again.

And after three years, when the winter was ebbing away and spring was fighting to reconquer the Dales, there was suddenly quiet. The machines had departed, the scarred earth had been turfed over and repaired, the water flowed, calm as honey, through the grey stone channel hidden two yards down amongst the grass and the sheep droppings, and the plover's and lark's nests.

The protesters had of course long departed and moved on to their next crusade, having achieved their aim. We threw a Guy Fawkes farewell party for them - huge bonfire and barbecue and booze, and their own makeshift band blasting the night away, amidst singing and laughter and exploding fireworks. We were sad to see them go. We all promised to stay in touch, but probably never would. They said they would be hiring holiday boats when the canal opened, and would see us then, but probably went instead to Ibiza or St Ives or the Greek Islands. They were passing spirits on the wind.

The Collins's and their entourage all came for the opening and the christening of the first barge's passage. George and his wife were there, and Garrick their project manager, who had been almost a local resident during the construction. And, surprisingly, Martin Collins, single, sun-tanned and casual, and looking a lot happier than when I had last seen him. Presumably he thought I was ignorant of his one-night fling with my wife. The two of them exchanged awkward greetings, but then kept well away from each other. I had forgiven him. It was from another era, another world. And if he was now saving this one, well good for him.

Several of the locals rolled up for the event too, such as big Fred the vet, and Mike Foster, my neighbour, and Sergeant Jack, and even Robbie, the barman from the King's Arms. Sir Peter Coverley arrived in his Bentley with Frank Carter, oozing patrician satisfaction. Vincent and Audrey, the organisers of the protesters, arrived, though whether they considered the occasion a victory or a defeat, I wasn't quite sure. And there was a fair flock of villagers who had somehow got wind of the occasion.

There were quite a crowd of us, strung across the wide cattle bridge that spanned the channel, and along the narrow tow path beside it. And when, after a lengthy wait in the chilly afternoon, a long dark shape slowly chugged towards us from the distant lock at the edge of Brad Faulkner's land, a burst of applause and clapping went up.

It wasn't much of a craft - bulky and squat, half submerged, like a giant seal nosing tentatively through unknown waters, and at this experimental stage bearing only a few of the priceless monoliths that it was built for. But to many there it represented a victory as significant as any that ended a military conflict.

Slowly, slowly, its ungainly bulk oozed its way tight between the banks and beneath our bridge, its half cargo of pale blocks squatting complacent in its belly. At the tiller, its captain - a sea-capped veteran of the oceans by the look of him - acknowledged the applauding throng with regal salutes. In the bows stood the mooring lad, with Danny beside him, grinning like a pop star. George Collins had suggested he be invited to go along for the ride, and of course Danny had jumped at it. He had already abandoned trains and cars for his studies of canal boats and their provenance. He probably knew more about them than Brunel.

George himself now clapped me on the shoulder, and said, 'We've made history today, Roger. It's been a long haul, but we got there in the end. There's always a way if you can find it.'

I nearly said, there should have been easier bloody ways, but I didn't.

I bought a new tractor, a new hay baler, and extended the ten acre meadow to twenty acres. I bought Lily her own racehorse foal, which she reared and trained at her stud. I bought my father a giant TV on which he watched the races, and the soaps, and for some reason cookery programs. I bought Danny a mini-buggy, which he used to roam around the farm on, within strict safety limits. He would ride it to the canal bridge, and spend hours there, logging with minute precision every barge and every holiday boat that passed underneath.

I didn't buy Annie and me a helicopter, but I bought us a small apartment in an old house in the shade of York's giant Minster, and we used it for culture trips to the city - galleries and theatres and nice restaurants. I got to quite enjoy them. We occasionally went to London for the odd 'dirty weekend' as she called them. And we went more often to Cornwall for holidays, and even flew to Venice and Vienna and Barcelona. I realised that I had led a very narrow existence.

Meanwhile, the toll money from the barges flowed in a steady trickle, whilst their cargoes built lofty edifices far away from us.

I could have retired if I'd wanted to. But farmers don't retire until they can't get out of bed.

The only thing that didn't change was the land. It ignored the minor scar that now ran across its face. It unfurled and slept and soared and snarled and sang, just as it had always done. It lived and breathed and waited for the end of creation, knowing it would be there long after we had all departed. It cared nothing for us, even as we cared for it.

ABOUT THE AUTHOR

Robin Hawdon's career has spanned many aspects of the arts - playwright, novelist, actor (who came near to being James Bond), stage producer, theatre director.

As a playwright, his plays have been produced in over forty countries, with major productions in London, New York, Chicago, Paris, Berlin, Bonn, Warsaw, Tel Aviv, Sydney, Johannesburg, Russia, Scandinavia, Italy, etc.

Robin's wife of over forty years, Sheila, is a psychotherapist and writer. They have two writer daughters, four grand-children, and homes in Bath, the South of France and Australia.

ROBIN'S OTHER BOOKS - available on Amazon and all major outlets.

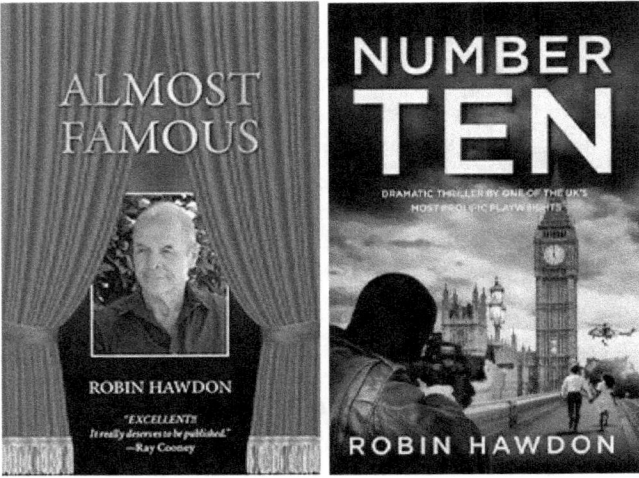

Sign up on Robin's website to receive his regular newsletter for all writers, readers, show-biz followers, and general political arguers. And also for his writer's blog.'How To Write'.
www.robinhawdon.com

www.ingramcontent.com/pod-product-compliance
Lightning Source LLC
Chambersburg PA
CBHW060930180626
46817CB00004B/1471